VILL

# VILE

FACES OF EVIL

DEBRA WEBB

PINK
HOUSE
PRESS

Copyright © 2014 Debra Webb, Pink House Press
Edited by Marijane Diodati
Cover Design by Kendel Flaum

PINK HOUSE PRESS
WebbWorks
Huntsville, Alabama

First Edition March 2014

ISBN 10: 0615938140
ISBN 13: 9780615938141

"For the vile person will speak villainy,
and his heart will work iniquity…"
~Isaiah 32:6

# CHAPTER ONE

SIXTH AVENUE FLOWER + GIFTS
BIRMINGHAM, ALABAMA
MONDAY, AUGUST 30, 10:30 A.M.

Ellen Gentry was mad as hell. She had worked at this floral shop for five years and not once had she called in sick. If her name was on the schedule, she was here—unless, of course, she was in the hospital or the morgue.

Apparently, she was the only employee with proper work ethics. Too bad her paycheck didn't reflect her dedication. She'd had to run around like a chicken with its head chopped off to fill this morning's orders all by herself. Nearly every one had been for an anniversary—not that she was complaining about that part. Anniversary arrangements were good for business and almost always included generous tips. Husbands, even the not so nice ones, typically went all out for that special celebration. A big old bouquet of flowers could get a guy out of hot water faster than almost anything.

Ellen placed the final arrangement in the walk-in cooler and breathed a sigh of relief. "Done."

It wasn't brain surgery, but her work gave her a sense of accomplishment. Speaking of surgery, she wouldn't mind snagging a doctor. There were plenty of them in Birmingham. She smoothed a hand over her hair and straightened her apron. These black slacks and white blouse were her favorites. They fit exactly right. She'd added a nice little red scarf as an accent. Looking her best wasn't just something she did for work. It never hurt to showcase her assets especially since all those husbands would be coming in to pick up their orders. Married guys were always telling their single friends about hot chicks they ran into. She looked pretty good even if she was about to turn thirty. There was still time to land a husband.

"Before all the good ones are gone," she grumbled. *Or maybe they already are.*

Time for a break—if she could find her drink. A quick survey of the counter and she spotted her Coke Zero right where she'd left it behind the cash register.

As she guzzled what she fondly called her coffee in a can, a frown scrunched up her brow. Why was that child still standing on the sidewalk outside the shop? The traffic was lighter now that the morning commute was over, but there were still plenty of cars whizzing along Sixth Avenue.

Ellen tossed the empty can into the trash and wandered to the door. The little blond haired girl had been standing in that same spot for going on an hour. Where in the world were her parents?

Some people were so stupid they didn't deserve to be parents. Ellen pushed through the door and the bell jingled overhead. The hot, humid air enveloped her instantly. It was going to be another scorcher. A few steps outside the door and she was already sweating.

The little girl didn't turn around. She stared out at the street as if she were lost. Was someone supposed to pick her up? Had a parent dropped her off and then driven away? How crazy was that?

"Hey there." Ellen crouched down, putting herself at eye level with the little girl who couldn't possibly be older than four. "What's your name, sweetie?"

The child turned to Ellen and then drew back in fear. Her little face was red from crying. "Don't be afraid," Ellen said gently. "Where's your momma?"

The child just stared at her without saying a word. A piece of plain white paper had been folded and fastened to her pink dress with a big safety pin. Ellen reached for the note. Surprisingly, the child held still as she removed it.

This was totally spooky. Ellen's heart beat faster as she unfolded the paper. The words there were formed with letters cut out from the newspaper and pasted together. "What in God's name?" She read the lone statement again.

*Take me to Deputy Chief Jess Harris.*

# CHAPTER TWO

Deputy Chief Jess Harris stared at the photos lying on her desk. Rory Stinnett and Monica Atmore. The two women had never met and had nothing in common other than being tall and gorgeous with dark hair—until now. Now, they shared something ugly and deadly. They were both hostages of the vile serial killer known as the Player.

Jess closed her eyes for a long moment. Eric Spears, the Player, had not contacted her since texting Monica's photo on Saturday. *We're waiting for you.*

The Joint Task Force investigating the case had nothing except what Spears had given them. It was as if he didn't really exist… except he did. Dozens of people, primarily women, were dead by his hand. Spears had touched Jess. He had stood toe to toe with Dan and stabbed him, leaving him for dead.

Shuddering, Jess forced away the memories. Spears was determined to murder innocent people

4

and to destroy all that Jess cared about until he acquired what he wanted: *Her.*

At this point, she might have gladly given him what he wanted to stop him, but fate had taken that choice from her. She was pregnant with Dan's child. Protecting herself was the only way to protect this child.

Jess had loved Dan Burnett since she was a teenager. No matter that they'd lived a thousand miles apart for two decades, she had never really stopped loving him. A weary smile tugged at her lips. He hadn't stopped loving her either. Both had simply been too hardheaded to admit it. So here they were twenty years later, ready to give a life together a second chance. They might actually have a happily ever after if the monster at the top of the evil scale obsessed with Jess failed. Problem was, the only way to ensure he didn't succeed was to find him.

The local police in more than one state, in addition to the Federal Bureau of Investigation as well as Interpol, were looking for him with no luck so far.

"CNN and Fox News picked up Coleman's story," Sergeant Chet Harper announced.

Jess blinked and pushed away the troubling thoughts about Spears. The members of her team were gathered at their desks. Since they hadn't caught a case this morning, she'd asked all four to focus on going over everything that had happened related to Spears since Jess's return to Birmingham six weeks ago. Not that she expected they would find anything new, but it never hurt to take another look.

Harper turned up the sound on the flat panel television that hung above their empty case board. The Special Problems Unit office was nothing more than one large room, but it served their needs for the time being. SPU was the newest unit in Birmingham's Police Department, and Jess felt privileged to be in charge. Her team, though small, was the best.

The reporter droned on about the escalating events in Birmingham, Alabama. A clip of Gina Coleman's expose on Eric Spears had Jess holding her breath. She'd seen the whole story on the local news last night. Gina, Birmingham's most beloved and highest rated investigative journalist, had done a good job. No wonder she'd won all those awards. She'd informed Jess this morning that the feedback from the community was tremendous and mostly supportive of Jess's situation. Since returning to her hometown, Jess had vacillated between the hero who'd come home to serve the city of Birmingham and the pariah determined to destroy it.

"I'm sure Mayor Pratt is loving this," Jess grumbled. The man had been trying to find a way to be rid of her since Dan offered her the position of deputy chief of SPU. Trouble was Jefferson County's Sheriff's department had been in on the deal. Since SPU was funded by Sheriff Griggs and Jefferson County as well as by the city of Birmingham, Pratt didn't have the final say.

Unfortunately, that left Dan in the middle to take the heat from the mayor and his allies. Jess couldn't help wondering if Dan had experienced any second thoughts about offering her the job.

The memory of the two of them rushing from the early morning fire at his home just a few days ago had her lungs burning for air and her heart thundering with remembered panic. An image of the headstone with Dan's name on it that Spears had delivered to Oak Hill Cemetery the day before the fire floated before her eyes next. Yet another piece of evidence indicative of his determination.

She could not allow Spears to destroy Dan.

When two celebrity detectives were brought on screen to dissect the situation, Jess had seen enough. She pushed out of her chair. "I need some air."

Three of the four members of her team immediately stood in reaction to her announcement. Jess sighed. This was her life at the moment. She couldn't even go to the ladies room without an escort.

Noticeably, the only person in the room who didn't react was Lori Wells. Lori was struggling with guilt over Friday's double suicide. Jess couldn't make her see that no one could have anticipated what happened. At some point, they were going to talk again. Somehow, Jess intended to get it through Lori's head that she hadn't done anything wrong. So far, nothing anyone said had reached her.

Harper and Cook as well as the newest member of their team, Lieutenant Clint Hayes, all waited for Jess to make the next move. In the background, the onscreen detectives bandied about her name and that of her worst nightmare.

How in the hell did she end all this?

She held up her hands in surrender. "Never mind." She turned to Harper. "Would you turn that off, please?"

"Yes, ma'am." Harper tapped the remote.

Silence filled the room with the four of them standing there as if waiting for some announcement they all knew wouldn't come. Lori sat hunched over her laptop not even looking up in the wake of the abrupt silence.

"We should…" Jess wasn't sure what she intended to say next, but she needed to say something.

Her cell phone broke into its old-fashioned ringtone saving her the trouble of deciding on a course of action for the moment. She reached for the phone and smiled at Dan's handsome face. Hearing his voice about now would be good. She accepted the call and turned to stare out the window behind her desk. "Hey." Behind her, chairs rolled and squeaked as the men in the room reclaimed their seats.

"I'm at a floral shop a few blocks from the office, Jess. Harper should be getting a call with the exact location."

As he said the words, Harper gave his usual greeting in answer to a call. Jess's pulse kicked into a faster rhythm. "What's going on?" She held her breath, waiting for news of another abduction or murder. *God, when would this end?*

"There's been a delivery." Dan hesitated before going on, those brief seconds ratcheting up the tension threatening to explode inside her. "We can't be sure Spears or one of his associates has anything to do with this, but—"

"I'll be right there." No need for him to say more. The tone of his voice warned it was a bad situation. Jess ended the call without saying goodbye. Her heart was already burgeoning in her throat.

"Ready, ma'am?"

Jess met Harper's gaze, then she nodded. "Let's go, Sergeant." To the others, including Hayes who looked ready to tag along, "Keep going over the details, especially last week's murders. If we missed anything related to Spears, I want to know."

Jess squared her shoulders. Whatever waited for her at that floral shop, she would be damned if she'd allow Spears this much control over her actions or her feelings.

As she and Harper exited the building, her fury built until she was scarcely able to contain it. She refused to be a prisoner of this SOB. She would not live in constant fear as he wanted. He relished the terror his victims experienced. It made him stronger.

She would not give him the satisfaction.

SIXTH AVENUE FLOWER
GIFTS, 12:01 P.M.

Both ends of the block on the street in front the floral shop had been cordoned off. Three BPD cruisers, as well as an ambulance, lined the curb in front of the shop. Dan's SUV was parked between two of the cruisers. Another car Jess didn't recognize sat amid the fray.

"What the hell happened here?" Jess shook her head. Harper hadn't been told any specifics, only the location.

Harper eased to the curb a good distance behind the ambulance. "We'd have more units on site if there'd been a shooting."

Absolutely. Jess surveyed the official vehicles. "No coroner's wagon, so I'm assuming we don't have a body."

Harper hummed his agreement. "No crime scene unit either. But we have a crowd of curious folks along with your rabid media fans." He sent Jess a smile that didn't quite make it to his eyes.

Jess groaned. A dozen or so people waited outside the police perimeter hoping for a chance to see the show. Testing the boundaries of that same perimeter and the patience of the cops vested with the duty of protecting it, reporters and cameramen from the local stations shouted questions and Jess hadn't even opened her door.

"Lucky me," she grumbled as she reached for the door handle.

Harper was out of the SUV and at her door before she had it fully open. He shielded her from the crowd as they rounded the vehicle and crossed the sidewalk.

"Were you and Eric Spears lovers?" one of the newshounds shouted.

Standing in the vee made by Harper's body and the open door to the shop, Jess stalled.

"Ignore him, ma'am."

It took about five seconds before she could act on Harper's sage advice, but she managed. When the door closed behind them with a jingle, she dismissed her annoyance with the media to focus on the place and whatever trouble lay within these walls.

Inside, a lone uniform was stationed at the door. Green potted plants and artificial flower arrangements lined the shelves of the shop. Ceramic crosses along with a few angel statues provided other gift options. Behind the counter, an officer was taking the statement of a young woman. Her back was turned to the door and she didn't bother looking to see who had entered. The officer nodded to Jess, but quickly shifted his attention back to the woman in the white blouse. Apparently, everyone else was in the rear of the shop. There was probably a storeroom and a walk-in cooler for the fresh flowers.

Floral shops always smelled like funerals to Jess. It wasn't that she didn't love flowers. She did. Yet there was something about the scents in a floral shop that she would always associate with death. Like the peace lilies she truly disliked. Vivid memories of standing in a shop very much like this one while her Aunt Wanda haggled with the owner for a wreath were forever etched across Jess's psyche. Their parents had just died and she and Lil were in a daze. Wanda hadn't been able to afford a decent wreath for her own sister's funeral.

"This way, Chief."

Jess hauled her head out of the past and belatedly wondered if they needed shoe covers and gloves.

Evidently, Harper saw the question in her eyes since he added, "No need for shoe covers or gloves. Nothing happened inside the shop."

That explained everything, she mused. Dan hadn't given her any details either, but then she had ended the call rather abruptly. "Thank you, Sergeant."

Harper escorted her across the retail space and through a door that opened into a short corridor. Another door marked "cooler" was to her left. On the right was an employees' restroom. Beyond those doors, the corridor opened into a storeroom. Shelves packed with floral supplies flanked the large room that appeared to be about twice the size of the front retail space. Dan and two more officers were huddled around a large worktable in the center of the room.

Dan met Jess's gaze and motioned for her to join them. As she moved closer, Jess could see that one of the officers, a woman, was talking to… a *child* seated on the table.

Jess moved into the huddle. The little girl had long blond hair. She couldn't have been more than four or five years old. Her cheeks were rosy and her brown eyes looked red from crying. She seemed relatively calm now. A pink dress with a white lacy collar and matching white sandals had Jess picturing her own child at that age. If the baby turned out to be a girl, there would be plenty of lace and pink dresses. Lil would see to that.

*Not the time, Jess.*

"Carry on, Officer Rice," Dan said, drawing Jess's attention to him. He ushered Jess into the farthest corner of the supply room.

"What's going on?" This was a crime scene but not really? The area had been cordoned off and cops were everywhere but no crime scene techs and no protective wear. Didn't make a lot of sense. "Is the woman out front the mother? Where's the father?"

Dan shook his head. "We don't know who the parents are. We don't even know who the child is. She hasn't said a word."

Jess frowned, scrubbed at her furrowed forehead with the back of her hand. "Did she just wander into the shop?" If that were the case, there was probably a dead body around here somewhere after all, or a missing person at the very least. Her frown deepened. This wasn't Spears's MO. This couldn't be him. Even as the words filtered through her brain, the knowing look in Dan's eyes chilled her blood.

"She was waiting on the sidewalk outside," Dan explained. "The clerk noticed her and went out to see if she was okay. There was a note pinned to her dress."

Jess didn't need a crystal ball to predict the rest. "I take it the note was addressed to me." Outrage rushed through her.

Dan reached into the pocket of his elegant silk suit jacket. No matter that it was hot as blazes outside, the man always dressed impeccably. Even with all that was going on, Jess resisted the urge to smile. He was ever the statesman. The charcoal suit looked good on him. A blue shirt and darker blue tie set off the color of his eyes. From the moment she'd first met Daniel Burnett at seventeen she had been mesmerized by him. He was handsome, charming, and so very kind. How could she have been so fortunate to have him still waiting for her after all this time? His three failed marriages notwithstanding, of course. To be fair, she had a failed marriage of her own.

He passed her the evidence bag. Part of her didn't want to look. It was easier not to see, but that choice wasn't hers to make. She accepted the piece of paper enclosed in the plastic evidence bag. She read it twice, the words stealing away the warmth and hope being near Dan always prompted.

*Take me to Deputy Chief Jess Harris.*

Jess turned to look at the little girl. *Please don't let this be a sign that he knows.* If Spears had learned of her pregnancy, he would use that vulnerability against her.

Her second thought was the child's mother could be the third hostage being held by the monster. The child might very well be the notification he loved providing to rattle the family and friends of his latest victim.

"A representative from Child Services in on the way."

Dan's words nudged her from the painful musings. Jess nodded before moving back to the worktable where Officer Rice spoke softly to the child, reassuring her with kind words. Jess took a picture of the little girl with her phone. She stared at Jess but didn't seem to mind.

"Hello," Jess said. The little girl looked up at her and Jess smiled. "I'm Deputy Chief Jess Harris. What's your—"

The little girl abruptly held out her arms toward Jess.

Startled, Jess looked to Dan.

"Excuse me, Chief."

Jess turned to the officer.

"I think she wants you to pick her up." Rice shrugged, embarrassed or uncertain if she'd overstepped her bounds. "I have a three year old at home."

"But I..." Jess hoped she didn't look as startled by the suggestion as she felt.

"Something about you makes her feel safe," Rice suggested.

Feeling way out of her comfort zone, Jess's attention settled on the little girl whose arms were still outstretched. Jess smiled, shifted her bag higher on her shoulder, and tentatively scooped the little girl into her arms. Her small legs went around Jess's waist, and her little head went against Jess's shoulder. With the emotional vise that had clamped around her chest, it was all Jess could do to draw in her next breath.

Someone somewhere would be frantically looking for this child.

Unless they were missing… or *dead*.

# CHAPTER THREE

Jess tried three times to hand the little girl over to Officer Rice. The child was having no part of it. Each time Jess attempted to put her down or hand her off, she screamed at the top of her lungs.

Harper stood by stoically, but Jess didn't miss the amusement glittering in his eyes. Like the officer, Harper had a three year old of his own. Not that his experience was helping in the least little bit right now. Dammit.

Desperate, Jess turned to Dan with a questioning look. He shrugged and reached for the little girl.

She whimpered and held onto Jess more tightly.

Jess sagged with defeat. "Fine. I'll just hang onto her for now."

As if the good Lord decided to take pity on Jess, a woman entered the storeroom, the heels of her leather pumps clicking on the tile floor. Before she said a word, her stiff posture and polyester blend suit announced she was from Child Services. Or maybe it was the stern expression.

Considering a woman in her position witnessed all manner of child abuse, who wouldn't wear some form of armor?

"Lois Wettermark, Jefferson County Child Services investigator." She looked from Dan to Jess and then to the child. "We still don't have a name?"

Jess shook her head. "She's not talking."

Wettermark walked straight up to Jess and reached for the little girl. The moment Wettermark's hands landed on her, the child started to wail. The investigator manufactured a smile about as fake as the one Jess had been shoring up all morning. "This sort of reaction isn't unusual. No need to be concerned, Chief. She'll be fine. You can let her go now."

"Okay." Despite the child's desperate attempts and the wailing, Jess relinquished her hold on the little girl. Oddly, her entire being felt bereft somehow at the loss. Maybe it was just the little girl's obvious unhappiness. More likely, it was hormones. If Jess survived the first trimester, she might make it through this pregnancy.

"If someone can bring my car around to the back," Wettermark suggested, "perhaps I can avoid the prying eyes of the press on our way out."

"Sergeant, would you see to that, please?" Jess instructed.

"Right away." Harper took the woman's keys and headed out.

Jess wished she were going with Harper. The way the little girl looked at her, reached for her was tearing at her heart. Jess scrubbed at her brow again and looked away. Dan appeared as unsettled as she felt. Though she doubted either of them felt as unhappy about this as the little girl did.

*Focus, Jess.* "I'd like to interview the clerk when... this is finished."

Dan nodded.

Wettermark's efforts to cajole the child continued to fall on deaf ears. Jess hated to stand here and do nothing.

Finally, she couldn't take it anymore. She walked over to the other woman and reached for the child. The little girl's wails quieted as she stretched toward Jess, making her heart ache all the harder. "Why don't I hold her for a minute?"

Wettermark shook her head. "That'll just make leaving more difficult for her, Chief Harris. It would be best if you went into the other room. You may remind her of someone she knows and that could be upsetting her."

Jess didn't see how her presence would be upsetting since the child stopped crying whenever she held her. Then again, she had little or no experience with children. What did she know? Obviously, everyone in the room, except maybe Dan, knew more than she did about the subject. "Well, all right then."

As wrong as it felt, Jess made her way to the front of the shop. Every step was a monumental exercise in self-control. She didn't dare glance back. Apparently, she had a lot to learn when it came to children.

If this was any indication of her nurturing side, she was doomed.

"It doesn't get any easier."

"Excuse me?" Jess turned to the officer who'd followed her. She hadn't realized Rice was right on her heels.

"Whenever a child is involved in something like this it's hard." She hugged herself as if she felt a sudden chill. "I've been a part of dozens of situations where kids are abandoned or left behind after a tragedy, and it doesn't get any easier."

"I don't usually work with children." *And I'm pregnant,* Jess wanted to shout. Her emotions were untrustworthy. Everything felt personal and too difficult. She was used to analyzing the details of a killer's work. Her job rarely involved children unless they were missing or deceased. She'd had a case a few weeks ago involving a young boy but not this young. This was uncharted territory on more than one level.

"I've been watching you on the news," Rice said. "Your story is very inspiring. It's an honor to have the opportunity to work with you."

The smile Jess managed this time was genuine. "Thank you."

Maybe Gina Coleman was right when she said the world needed to know the whole story about the past few months. Jess had given that interview over the weekend. For the first time since returning to Birmingham, she'd told someone besides Dan the story of how her life had come to be entangled with a serial killer.

Rice hitched her thumb toward the storeroom and the still wailing little girl. "I'll just make sure everything's okay in there."

Jess gave her a nod and shifted her attention to the clerk. Ellen Gentry sat on a stool behind the counter. She had wrung her hands until Jess was reasonably sure the skin was chapped.

"Miss Gentry, I'm Deputy Chief Jess Harris."

Gentry nodded. "You're that lady from the news." Gentry jerked her head in what was probably a nod. "The one the serial killer is after."

Wasn't being a celebrity fun? "That's me. I'd like to ask you a few questions, if you don't mind." The sobbing in the back room faded, signaling the little girl was gone, and somehow making Jess feel sad. *Damned pregnancy hormones.*

"Like I told the other cop, I don't really know anything. I noticed her out there and got worried."

Jess pulled her pad and pencil from her bag and flipped to a clean page. "Did you notice her more than once?"

Gentry seemed to think about that question for a moment, then she nodded. "I had a bunch of orders to fill, but I remember glancing outside and noticing her there. A good while later, after I'd filled all those orders, I noticed her again. That's when I got concerned." She glanced outside. "I hope no one's tried to come for their order yet. I can't afford to have my business being turned away."

"We'll be finished in a few minutes," Jess assured her. "Would you say you went out to check on her a half hour or an hour after the first time you noticed her on the sidewalk?"

"Close to an hour I think, but I can't say for sure."

"What time do you open the shop?"

"I get here about eight-thirty and I open the doors at nine." She fidgeted with her nails, picking at a cuticle. "I would've checked on her sooner. I had no idea her parents had just dumped her out there."

"You couldn't have known," Jess offered. "Did you come in through the front or the back this morning?"

"The back." Gentry's right foot started to pat the air. She was nervous or upset. Understandable. "Something like twenty minutes later when I unlocked the front door, I walked out onto the sidewalk to pick up a McDonald's cup someone had tossed and she wasn't there then."

"You unlocked the front door around nine?"

Gentry nodded.

"As you went about filling your orders, did you notice anyone passing by? Did anyone come inside and place an order or just browse?"

The clerk wagged her head from side to side. "All my orders were made by phone. I had a couple from yesterday that were done on the Internet. No one came in the shop this morning."

"Did you notice anyone on the sidewalk when you went outside to see about the little girl? Maybe someone who had just passed your shop? Someone walking away?"

Gentry shrugged. "Sorry. I didn't see anyone but I wasn't really looking."

Most people didn't. "Did the little girl say anything at all to you?"

"No. She wouldn't tell me her name. She just looked at me. I thought maybe she was mute until she started crying back there."

"She wasn't crying when you found her?" Jess remembered the little girl's eyes being red as if she'd been crying.

"I think maybe she'd been crying, but she wasn't when I went out there. She started crying when the cops—" she cleared her throat "—when the guys in uniforms showed up."

"I'd like you to write down your address and contact numbers for me." Jess passed her the notepad and pencil. "If anyone calls or stops by and asks anything at all or even mentions the child, I want you to let me know." Jess placed her business card on the counter. "Watch for anyone suspicious hanging around outside. Call us if you feel anything at all is out of the ordinary."

Gentry handed the pad back to Jess and picked up the card. "You think they'll come back for her?"

"It's not likely but we can hope."

"You think that serial killer took the little girl's mother?"

Jess wished she could say no, but the truth was she had no idea. Eric Spears was capable of anything. "I'm sure we'll have some answers soon."

Thankfully, two of the officers had disbursed the crowd outside the shop. Jess doubted the reporters had gone very far, but she had a job to do. That job included having a look around outside. But first, she had an idea she hoped might help them learn what happened. She went in search of Dan. He and Harper were still in the storeroom. Probably discussing strategies for keeping Jess off the streets—despite Dan's outward reasonableness about her work of late.

She hated, hated, hated this incessant need for everyone around her to protect her. She could protect herself.

"Harper and I are going outside to have a look around," she said to Dan. "Can you check with your source and find out if the area in front of the shop is on the city surveillance system the mayor had installed?"

That would be a huge break. The mayor had had a system installed several years ago to monitor certain downtown streets, but not all areas and angles were covered. If they were really lucky the shop would be.

"I've already made the call," Dan let her know. He glanced around, clearly reluctant to go. "I'll drop the note off at the lab. Anything else you need?"

Jess shook her head firmly. "I've got this. You go be Chief of Police."

He gave her a little two-fingered salute. "All right. I'm out of here."

As he passed, he squeezed her hand. That simple touch sent heat surging through her. No matter how wrong things between them had gone in the past, she was so grateful for what they had now. It was going to take them working together to get through this.

"Looks like the coast is clear outside, ma'am," Harper said.

"Thank you, Sergeant. Let's see what we can find."

Outside they walked the block and found what she'd fully expected. Nothing. There were a good number of offices and shops in the area. They started on the end of the block nearest the floral shop and began a grid search. The first officers on the scene had already canvassed the area, but Jess had questions the officers might not have thought to ask.

Did any of the businesses have security cameras that might have picked up anyone walking along the sidewalk? Had anyone with a child stopped in that morning? Did anyone recognize the child in the photo she'd taken? A resounding chorus of no's were the only answers.

Her cell rang and Jess dug it from her bag. *Dan.* "Hey." She hoped he had good news for her.

"The cameras got something. It's being sent to your office right now."

Anticipation mounted. "Great. Thanks. I'll keep you posted." Jess tucked her phone back into her bag and turned to Harper. "We may have a lead from the city's security cameras. They're sending a copy to the office."

"Looks like we have trouble headed this way." Harper nodded toward his SUV. "Stay behind me, ma'am."

Jess groaned when she recognized the TV reporter, Gerard Stevens. She did not like the man. He was one of those guys who would do anything to get ahead, even if it meant stepping on his own grandmother's toes. He'd taken two major pot shots at Dan and the department already. Jess considered herself fair game since she was the one to bring Spears to Birmingham. Dan, on the other hand, didn't deserve any of this.

"Chief Harris," Stevens proclaimed in that big, deep, condescending voice of his, "is it true that Spears remains in contact with you?"

Harper stayed between Jess and the cameraman shadowing Stevens.

"Didn't you watch Gina Coleman's story?" Jess asked, rubbing in the fact that Stevens didn't scoop the big story.

He smiled. "Is that a yes, Chief?"

They had arrived at Harper's SUV. He'd opened the door. Jess could have gotten in without saying another word, but she just couldn't help herself. "That's a no comment, sir. If you want the facts on Eric Spears, you should check with Gina Coleman."

Satisfied she had spoiled his day, Jess settled into the passenger seat. It felt good to give it to a guy like Stevens. She suspected that might be the only highlight of her day.

VILE

The team gathered around the monitor and watched as the video from the city's security cameras played on the screen a fourth time. A woman in jeans, a nondescript t-shirt, and sneakers walked hand in hand with the little blonde girl. It was impossible to get a good description of the woman. Her hair was tied back and covered with a scarf. She wore large sunglasses to shield her eyes and a good portion of her face. And she puffed on a cigarette.

"She doesn't move like a runner," Lori noted.

"Not enough muscle mass for that," Hayes agreed.

The woman was practically skin and bone. The tight fit of the jeans and the tee as well as her bare arms confirmed that assessment. Her lips were painted a deep Marilyn Monroe red.

"I can't tell if she has dark hair or it's just that black scarf," Cook said. "Her eyebrows are dark. That could mean her hair is too."

"She was careful," Harper agreed. "She didn't want anyone to recognize her. Then or now."

"I'm hoping she's in the database." Jess watched the woman kneel down and pin the note to the child's dress. Since she didn't wear gloves, there would be prints.

"Watch her lips," Lori said, "she's giving the kid final instructions."

Jess studied the woman's mouth as she spoke. There was no audio but Jess recognized part of what she said.

*Remember…*

"Remember," Lori said, echoing Jess's thought, "what…" She shook her head. "Let's see it again."

Cook hit backward search and then play.

"Remember," Lori said, "what move or…"

"Mommy," Jess said.

"Remember what mommy told you." Lori turned to Jess. "She's the kid's mother."

Jess nodded. "That's the way it looks to me."

"What kind of mother would leave her kid on the street like that?" Harper demanded.

"She's working for Spears," Hayes announced. His gaze collided with Jess's. "He's using the kid to send you a message."

Hayes was the only person in the room who knew Jess was pregnant. She understood exactly what he meant but she hoped he kept it to himself. Eventually, she wanted to share the news with her team—her friends. But she couldn't do that yet. They were already too protective of her. She could scarcely breathe much less investigate a case with them hovering. Learning this news would only double their efforts to keep her safe. Thankfully, Dan had been reasonable so far. At least as reasonable as he intended to be when it came to her safety.

"What does the kid have to do with Spears?" Lori challenged, that tension Jess had already noted between Hayes and the other male members of the team, apparently, extended to Lori as well.

"If he's trying to tell me something," Jess said, hoping Hayes would leave it at that, "I'm not getting the message."

Hayes shrugged. "Maybe he's using the mother as his next distraction. The way he used Ellis and the Man in the Moon before him."

It seemed Spears had decided the best way to get to Jess was to create enough diversions to keep the Birmingham PD running in a dozen directions. At least, that was Dan and Gant's theory. Supervisory Special Agent Ralph Gant was her former boss at Quantico. He was leading the Player Joint Task Force and he was convinced Jess was the ultimate target. Not that there was any question in anyone's mind about that theory.

There was nothing like being the obsession of a sociopathic serial killer.

"What about the footprints they do when a child is born?" Jess turned to Harper who was the only one in the room with a child. "Can they identify the little girl that way?"

"Depends on where she was born but I wouldn't count on it. Those footprints are primarily for the hospitals. To make sure the right baby goes home with the right mother. Most don't enter the footprints into a state wide or national database."

Something else to worry about. Jess had to find a doctor as soon as possible. Dan had made a few suggestions, which she appreciated. Selecting a doctor also determined which hospital would be used. Preferably one that ensured the right baby went home with her. On cue, her stomach roiled. The intense nausea she'd suffered last week had calmed down a little. Then again, last week might have been more about nerves and shock than morning sickness.

"Check with Child Services," she said to Harper. "I'd like to know the little girl's doing okay."

"On it." Harper retreated from the group and headed for his desk.

Lori followed suit without saying more.

"Cook and I are going out to pick up lunch," Hayes declared.

"We are?" Cook looked confused.

"We are," Hayes confirmed. "I could use some fuel." He looked directly at Jess as he said this.

"Text me your orders," Cook said as he followed Hayes out the door.

Jess hadn't even thought about lunch. Maybe she needed her team looking out for her more than she realized.

If distraction was what Spears was after at this stage in his game, she was falling right into his trap.

# CHAPTER FOUR

Dan waited for the other man to settle in before he began. He'd wrestled with this decision all weekend. As much as it pained him—no, scratch that—as much as it annoyed the hell out of him to have to do this, he wasn't a fool. At this point, it was more than obvious that he needed legal protection.

Despite being unspoken, the words were bitter on his tongue and heavy in his heart.

Frank Teller, Birmingham's top criminal defense attorney, leaned back in his chair and studied Dan. "It's been a while. How are the folks?"

Teller graduated high school with Dan. They'd played football together and done all the other stuff guys attending a small private school did. More importantly, they knew each other's deepest, darkest secrets from back in the day. Having that level of knowledge on a man could make him your best ally. Not that any of their secrets were worth much as leverage. A few peeping tom exploits and a couple of stolen mascot incidents. Whatever else they had shared, their time at Brighton Academy had ingrained a certain loyalty. Teller would do his best for a fellow alumnus.

After high school, they'd gone their separate ways. Dan had followed Jess to Boston and Teller had headed to Tennessee's Vanderbilt University. In time, they'd both returned to Birmingham.

"They're doing well. Dad retired after his heart attack, but he's doing great now." His father might object to that last part depending on how much trouble his wife was giving him. Katherine Burnett could make life... complicated. But she was Dan's mother and he loved her.

Teller nodded. "I see Annette from time to time. Did you hear she filed for divorce from Brandon? He's already engaged to someone else."

"I hadn't heard." Dan was so out of touch with everything and everyone—including the stepdaughter, Andrea, he still claimed in spite of the divorce from Annette. "Brandon's an ass. I'm glad she's moving on."

"I hear you've moved on as well," his old friend noted. "I remember Jess. She's all over the news these days. I guess she left Birmingham and made quite the name for herself in the FBI. Good for her."

Dan nodded. "She did. We're fortunate to have her in the department."

Teller studied him for a time before getting down to business. "Why don't you give me an overview of what's going on, and then we can best determine how we should proceed?"

"Three weeks ago one of my division chiefs went missing."

"Captain Ted Allen," Teller said. "Saw that on the news too."

"There were issues between him and Jess. We believe he made an attempt on her life just before he disappeared."

"What kind of attempt?"

"A car bomb."

Teller arched an eyebrow. "But that hasn't been proven?"

"The investigation is ongoing." Dan wasn't at liberty to say more on the subject at this time. The truth was he didn't have much more than that. "Just over a week ago his cell phone was found in my trash. I left the trashcan on the street on pick up day and somehow it was overturned. A pedestrian noticed the cell phone lying in the street and assumed someone had dropped it. Forensics later determined the cell had been inside my trashcan."

"Circumstantial at best," Teller argued.

No matter that he'd known that was the case, Dan felt some amount of relief at hearing an attorney say so. "Then last week Allen's wedding band was found in the grill I keep on my patio."

Teller turned up his hands. "Easily accessible. Anyone could have put it there."

"I've come under scrutiny in the investigation," Dan confessed. "That's as it should be under the circumstances. Since I was aware of the direction the investigation had taken, it looks suspicious that my house was basically destroyed by a fire. The fact that only days before the fire my security system was breached doesn't appear to matter." Dan held up a finger. "Also, I can't forget the report recently found in Allen's desk suggesting he intended to file a grievance against me. Somehow, that report was overlooked the first few times his office was searched."

"Someone's going to a hell of a lot of trouble to set you up, Dan." Teller searched his face. "You made any enemies lately?"

"None that I'm aware of." Dan exhaled a heavy breath. "I'm certain not every decision I make suits everyone in the department. But I can't fathom anything I've done to cause this sort of reaction."

"What about your choice to bring Jess Harris onboard? Was that decision well received?"

Though Dan understood the question was necessary, it still rankled that the man asked. "By most, I believe."

"Is there anyone who would like to have your job who perhaps thought they should have had it instead of you?" Teller shrugged. "The situation with Jess and this obsessed serial killer may have presented the opportunity needed to right that perceived wrong."

Dan had pondered that theory as well, but he didn't want to believe the one qualified man who'd been passed over would go to such extremes. He'd known Harold Black for more than twenty years. After a bumpy few weeks in the beginning, Harold had backed Dan up every step of the way in his position as chief.

Why would he turn on him now?

*Jess.*

Maybe. Certainly for some reason Harold disliked her. He'd been complaining about her from the very beginning.

"I don't believe this is an inside job, Frank." Dan wasn't ready to go there. "I honestly don't know who's behind it. On some level, it makes me feel better assuming Eric Spears has set this sequence of events into motion."

"Whoever it is," the attorney submitted, "he's doing a damned good job of pushing you into a corner." Teller clasped his hands in his lap and appeared to weigh the situation a moment before he continued. "Wherever the threat is coming from, you need to protect yourself, Dan. You need to start immediately. Based on what you've told me, the situation is escalating. We don't want to wait until you've been put on administrative leave or had charges filed against you."

Dan nodded. He felt ill. Was this really his life they were discussing? It seemed insane, but it was real. "I agree that we need to move quickly. I'm also thinking, in light of the fire, that maybe I need to get my affairs in order."

Teller frowned. "Are you talking about your estate? Are you feeling threatened on that level? If so, there are other precautions we need to consider."

Dan held up his hands. "With all that's occurred, I think it would be best." If anything happened to him, he wanted to ensure Jess and the baby would be well taken care of.

Teller passed a hand over his chin. "There's someone in my office who can handle your estate for you, *if* you prefer not to use your family attorney."

His family attorney was a lifelong friend of his parents. Dan was reasonably confident it would be best if he had a more objective voice handling his personal matters. "That would be very helpful."

"In that case," Teller stood and Dan did the same, "I'll have my assistant prepare the necessary documents of our agreement, and I'll see that my colleague contacts you about your private affairs."

Dan skirted his desk and shook his old schoolmate's hand. "I appreciate it, Frank. This is a difficult situation. I need someone I can trust without reservation in my corner." No one understood that necessity better than Frank. Though their pranks together had been basically harmless, Frank had gone too far once with his need to make a nemesis look bad. Dan had covered Teller's ass when no one else would. Frank owed him.

"Absolutely." Frank's eyes told Dan that he was remembering exactly how much he owed Dan. "You can count on me."

When his friend was gone, Dan moved to the window and stared out at the city he loved. He couldn't say how this was going to end. Whatever happened, he would not let Jess and their child down. A smile tugged at his lips. If their baby was a boy, he couldn't wait to teach him how to play football and to cheer for the best team in the nation, Alabama's Crimson Tide.

His heart melted at the idea of having a little girl who looked like Jess. There would be dance and piano lessons and eventually recitals. He blinked at the foolish emotions that blinded him for a moment.

No one was taking this happiness from him. He would see Eric Spears in hell first.

# CHAPTER FIVE

Jess placed the photo she'd printed of the little blonde girl on the case board. Harper had started a timeline of events. The best they could estimate, the woman had left the child between nine-fifteen and nine-thirty this morning. Lori and Cook were at the security company office reviewing the video feed recorded between eight and eleven this morning on every downtown camera in the system. It was a tedious task, but if they caught a glimpse of the woman who'd dropped off the child maybe they would at least learn the make of the vehicle she drove.

It was worth a shot.

Hayes was at his desk contacting hospitals in a hundred mile radius. Another monotonous job that likely wouldn't yield any results.

Clues in a case such as this were like finding the needle in the haystack. You had to sift through the numerous possibilities in hope of finding a single shred of evidence.

Approximately seven hours and counting. Why had no one reported the child missing?

A rap on the door preceded Deputy Chief Harold Black poking his head into the office. Jess worked up a smile although she would have preferred to demand what the hell he wanted. She was not happy with the man. Then again, she rarely was.

"Chief Harris," he said in that kind, we're-all-friends-here tone of his, "I need your help with the perp I have in interview room three."

Jess smoothed her hand down the front of her suit jacket. Very soon, she had to take the time to go shopping. Already she'd noticed her waistbands tightening. She'd had to hold her breath to zip this skirt this morning. "Certainly. I'll be right there."

Black opened the door a little wider. "I'll just wait and walk you down."

Lieutenant Hayes was at her side before Jess could respond. "I should join you. In case you need my assistance."

For a second, Jess weighed the prospect of telling both men that she was perfectly capable of walking wherever she wanted to go, but she opted not to waste her breath. Instead, she smiled at Hayes and said, "Good. You can carry my bag."

Without so much as a blink, he strode over to her desk and rounded up the big black leather bag she carried everywhere. Actually, it wasn't the original she'd bought herself for her fortieth birthday—that one had gone up in smoke with the fire at Dan's. This was one just like it. Sylvia Baron, Jefferson

County's associate medical examiner and a friend, had given it to Jess.

"Don't forget my phone," she reminded Hayes.

He grabbed the cell phone from her desk and hustled over to the door.

Jess turned to Black. "Lead the way."

As they exited, Jess glanced at Harper who smirked. Though Hayes was a damned fine addition to their team so far, he still had a way to go with fitting in. Simply because he outranked the others didn't make him more important to Jess or to the team. Somehow, he had decided that it was his job to stick to Jess. His eagerness was creating tension among the others. That annoyance, however, wasn't anywhere near the top of her priority list.

"We received a call this morning," Black explained as they headed for the elevators, "about a disturbance at one of the smaller homeless shelters in the area. When we arrived, the residents were in the street and the two men overseeing the facility were injured. One is still in the hospital. The other was treated and released."

"There was a murder?" Jess presumed so since Crimes Against Persons had caught the case. Though that division worked everything from assaults to murders, she suspected they were talking about a murder since Black was personally involved. He preferred having his hand in the higher profile cases.

He nodded. "A gruesome one with some unexpected similarities to a previous case involving Spears."

Jess stilled. "Why wasn't I called to the scene?"

They hesitated at the elevator and Black pressed the call button. "Let's not get ahead of ourselves now, Harris. I think this might be a copycat trying to get our attention. That's why I'm calling on you now."

The elevator doors opened and Jess moved inside. Waiting for the others to board gave her the few seconds she needed to get her irritation under control. About a minute of his condescending attitude and she was ready to punch the guy. "Why don't you tell me about the scene since you saw no need to show it to me?"

"One of the men who has been staying at the shelter for the past week dragged another of the residents, also male, into the bathroom and used a hacksaw in an attempt to cut off his hands and feet. He wasn't successful since the other residents discovered what he was doing before he finished. Unfortunately, he hit an artery or two and the victim expired at the scene."

"Has he given a statement?"

Black shook his head. "He wants to speak to you."

Judging by his tone and expression, Black wasn't too happy about the demand. If she'd had any question, his silence for the remainder of the trip to the interview room confirmed her suspicion. So this was why he'd bother to call on her at all.

"Lieutenant, you can watch with me," Black ordered, indicating the door to the viewing booth.

"I'd prefer to go in with Chief Harris. That's a violent perp in there. Her safety is—"

"I'll be fine." Jess removed her Glock from her bag and passed it to Hayes. "I'm certain Mister...?" She looked to Black.

"Terry Bellamy," Black supplied. "Sixty-eight years old, unmarried, no family in Birmingham."

"I'm certain Mr. Bellamy," Jess continued, "is properly restrained."

Black nodded. "He is indeed."

Obviously unhappy with her decision, Hayes didn't argue.

Jess was glad. She did not want to embarrass him in front of Black.

As she entered the interview room, Mr. Bellamy didn't look up. His clothes were disheveled and bloody. His hair was more gray than brown and sticking out every which way but right. His hands were cuffed behind his back and restraints had been secured around his ankles. He stared at the table as if he hadn't heard her come in or didn't want to acknowledge her presence. She settled her bag on the floor and took the seat opposite him. The smell of blood and filth was nearly overpowering.

"Hello, Mr. Bellamy. I'm Deputy Chief Jess Harris. Would you like to tell me what happened this morning?"

He lifted his head and stared directly at her. His face was marred by age, hopelessness, and a few bruises she suspected he'd sustained during his scuffle with the police. His eyes disturbed her the most.

Ghostly pale gray eyes filled with the harsh reality that he had long ago lost the war with his many demons.

"I didn't want to do it," he whispered, his words heavy with remorse.

"What did you do, Mr. Bellamy? I can't help you unless you tell me what happened."

He dropped his gaze again. His shoulders sagged with a heavy sigh. "I did it just the way he told me to. I hid the hacksaw in the bathroom. I waited until old Chuck was asleep, then I dragged him into the bathroom. He takes them pills to make him sleep so I knew he wouldn't give me no trouble."

"Who gave you these instructions?"

"It wasn't as easy as he said it'd be," Bellamy continued as if she hadn't spoken. "I 'bout wore my arm out and I still couldn't cut through the bone. Got blood everywhere. The cops told me Chuck was dead." He shook his head. "I didn't want to do it." His shoulders moved up and down in a listless shrug. "I shoulda never listened to that devil."

Jess held her breath. The odor was making her stomach churn. "Who told you to do this, Mr. Bellamy? Who gave you the hacksaw?" Her heart pounded twice for every second that passed before the man lifted his gaze to her once more.

"Spears," he said with a covert glance from side to side. "He's been watching me. Whispering in my ear. He's watching you too. He's coming for you. He told me so."

Jess willed her racing heart to slow. "How do you know it was Spears?" She kept his first name to herself. No matter that the attempt at removing the victim's hands and feet was reminiscent of an act committed by one of Spears's followers, this man may have heard about it on the street or in the news. He clearly suffered from a mental illness. The memory may have stuck in his head only to bob to the surface at a very bad time for the victim.

"What did Chuck do to make you want to hurt him, Terry?" Time to get personal. Make him feel as if she were on his side.

He shook his head. "He didn't do anything. He was just a bum like me." His mouth worked for a second before he went on. "I had to do it. Spears said if I didn't he'd torture me all the way to hell."

Jess chose a different tactic. "Mr. Bellamy, I still don't understand how you know the man who asked you to do this was Spears. Can you describe him? What color was his hair and eyes? How tall? Anything you can tell me will help."

"When they see the blood," Bellamy said, all inflection gone from his voice, "they will pass over you, and you shall not suffer death as his enemies are destroyed one by one."

Fear snaked around her chest and tightened. "Mr. Bellamy, is that from the Bible? Have you been studying the Good Book?"

The old man leaned forward ever so slightly, that troubled gaze boring into hers. "For you are *his*, now and forever."

How the hell could he know? The Vance sisters had chanted those words to Jess mere moments before committing suicide. None of that had been released to the media. This was—

Bellamy slammed his head against the table. Blood spurted from his nose.

Jess scrambled back too late to prevent blood from splattering her ivory suit jacket. She jumped out of her chair and reached for the man as he repeatedly bashed his head against the metal table. Her shouts for him to stop were ignored.

Black and Hayes rushed into the room and hauled him away from the table. Blood streamed down his face.

Jess froze for a second. All she could do was stare in disbelief at the poor man.

"Go," Black urged. "We need paramedics."

Jess bolted into action. She grabbed her bag and hurried out of the room to make the call.

When she had been assured the paramedics were en route, she leaned against the wall and went through the paces of calming herself. Her whole body shook with the receding adrenaline.

Was the monster really in Birmingham or was this another of his minions? Jess reached up and rubbed her forehead as hard as she could. Selma Vance had smeared Eric Spears's blood there. Jess shuddered at the memory.

Gant was wrong. Spears wasn't in hiding. He was here. Jess was certain of it.

THE GARAGE CAFE, TENTH
TERRACE SOUTH, 5:45 P.M.

Jess stared at the glass of Coke in front of her. She wished it were a triple shot of Tequila, and she didn't even like Tequila. Be that as it may, at the moment she could use anything to take the edge off.

Except she was pregnant and that couldn't happen.

She kept thinking about that poor homeless man. Why take advantage of the helpless? There was nothing like that in Spears's past MO. Maybe that vile act hadn't been Spears at all. Were his followers wreaking havoc on his behalf as a constant source of distraction to the BPD?

What about the little girl left on the street? Who would do such a thing? Unbelievable.

How could any mother desert her child? Obviously, Spears had set it up, but what could possibly have motivated the mother to go along? According to Child Services, the little girl showed no signs of physical abuse. Those brown eyes and all that long blond hair haunted Jess. That could be her little girl. A shudder quaked through her. Was that the point? Had Spears chosen this child for that reason? Did this move mean he knew Jess was pregnant?

She closed her eyes and shook her head. *Not going down that path*. They would eventually find out the child's name, and then maybe they could find the mother. The child still wasn't talking. Jess had called to check on her twice. The last time was shortly before she'd arrived to meet Buddy Corlew.

She'd taken a table as far from the entrance as possible. Hayes, damn him, was posted at the bar. He refused to stay outside. Jess hadn't even gone back to her office after the incident in the interview room. She'd had Hayes drive her straight here.

Frankly, she didn't know what she expected Corlew to do or say that would help, or even explain anything for that matter, but she needed to talk to him. There hadn't been a chance for them to catch up since his arrest on Friday. She felt so damned bad about that. If she hadn't asked him to help her out he likely wouldn't have been arrested.

This was insane. She shook her head. All of it.

As if her worrying had summoned him, Corlew waltzed into his favorite establishment. She'd chosen this place for that reason, plus it was off the beaten path. He waved to the bartender whom he likely knew by name. Corlew's long hair was secured in a ponytail as usual. The jeans looked as old as she knew for a fact he was. The Crimson Tide tee and leather vest along with the cowboy boots completed the I'm-redneck-and-I'm-proud-of-it attitude. His big black Charger would be parked outside. Buddy Corlew had been a showoff back in high school and that character flaw had followed him clear into middle age.

Sometimes, Jess wondered if she was out of her mind to trust him. But he'd built a sound reputation as a private detective. He'd been a cop before that. She doubted she would ever know the whole story about why he'd allowed the drinking and the sloppy police work to force Dan to fire him. Dan and Corlew were lifelong enemies—which made what she was doing even more complicated.

Corlew dragged out a chair at her table and dropped into it. "You know the last time I met you in a place like this my ass got busted."

Jess sipped her cola to wet her throat. "I feel bad about that. I really don't know exactly what happened. I was a little busy watching two young women blow their brains out."

He grimaced. "You do have a way of getting into tight spots, Jess."

"Yeah well that's my cross to bear, I guess." No more beating around the bush. "Who's your source inside the department?"

He shook his head. "You know I won't give you that." The bartender showed up with a frosty mug of beer and placed it in front of Buddy.

"You need anything else, man?"

"That'll do it." Buddy gave him a nod.

Jess waited until the man was out of earshot. "Can you still help me with Dan's situation?" She'd asked Buddy to look into who was framing Dan for Allen's disappearance.

Buddy took a long guzzle of beer, wiped his mouth with the back of his hand, and then leaned across the table. "I can help and I will. I ain't letting Danny boy go down for what we both know he didn't do."

"Is it Black?" Jess couldn't take the not knowing. She was already mad as hell at Black for just being himself.

Corlew shrugged. "I can't say for sure. I know the mayor's putting pressure on Black but I can't confirm he's the one making trouble for Dan. You have to be patient, Jess. These things take time."

She rolled her eyes. "Patience has never been one of my virtues, and I don't know how much time we have."

"Now that's the truth, sister." He lifted his beer to his lips once more.

Jess braced herself. "What about the other?" She'd also asked him to look into the accident that killed her parents. As much as she did not want to believe her Aunt Wanda's ridiculous tales about her mother's alleged fear of her father's associates, Jess couldn't deny that Wanda had filed a report with the police after their deaths. Then again, just because that part of Wanda's story was true didn't mean the rest was.

Whatever caused the accident thirty-two years ago, Jess needed to understand what had been going on with her parents—if anything. Maybe it was a lot of contrived BS from a woman who'd spent years drinking and drugging and God knows what else. Jess wanted the truth out one way or another. This thing with Spears had her second-guessing everything about her life.

"There was an investigation into the accident," Corlew said. "My source is attempting to get his hands on the case file. My arrest almost nailed him. They're watching him right now. He has to be careful."

"Why can't I pull the case file?" She'd been to records before. She and Lori had pulled the entire Man in the Moon case a couple of weeks ago.

Corlew made a noncommittal sound that was more grunt than anything else. "I don't know if that's such a good idea, kid. I should see that file before you do."

Oh hell. Now he was protecting her too! "If I had known there was a case file I would have pulled it already," she let him know in no uncertain terms. "The State Trooper's report was cut and dried. I obtained a copy of it years ago." She'd had no idea there was any sort of local investigation. How could Wanda not have told her this ludicrous story years ago?

*Maybe because you pretended she didn't exist until just recently.*

"Just promise me if you do that, we'll look at it together," Corlew urged.

"You've known me too long to doubt whether I can take care of myself." She and Corlew had grown up on the same side of the tracks. They'd both struggled, her in a carousel of foster homes and him with a drunk for a father and a mother who was afraid of her own shadow.

"Listen to me, kid." He reached across the table and squeezed her hand. "You and I know fate can throw your whole life for a loop. We've been there, done that. We've also learned it's a whole lot easier to get the job done with a friend than doing it all alone."

Well, she couldn't deny the truth in those words. As independent as she'd always been, she would be the first to admit these days that having a friend was better than not.

"All right. I'll have Lori pull the file, then you and I will go over it together."

"Lori can join us too. Give me someone to flirt with."

Jess kicked him under the table.

"Ouch!"

"You are not using one of my detectives to feed your immature fantasies."

Corlew laughed. "It was worth a try."

Jess worked at relaxing as she finished her Coke. By the time she got home Dan would already have been informed of the incident in the interview room. She'd have her hands full convincing him that she was never in any danger during the episode.

Besides, they had other things to talk about. Like when to tell her sister and his parents about the baby. Jess swallowed back a groan. She would rather walk on hot coals than tell Katherine Burnett that her first grandchild was on the way.

God help her.

# CHAPTER SIX

"Thank you, Lieutenant."

Hayes shifted into park. "You okay?"

Jess drew her bag onto her lap. How many times had she been asked that question in the past few weeks? Too many times to count. Was she okay in the truest sense of the word? Probably not. Was there a thing in the world this man could do about it? Definitely not. No need for him to be as miserable as she was about her current dilemma.

"I am." She smiled to cover the lie before reaching for the door. "I'll see you in the morning, Lieutenant."

"Night, Chief."

By the time she was out of the lieutenant's car, Dan was already headed down the stairs to greet her. Since the fire, they were living in the garage apartment she had rented from George Louis. The place was nice enough and in the kind of neighborhood to which Dan was accustomed. Forest Park wasn't Mountain Brook, but it was a respected and a historic neighborhood. Of course, the apartment was about the size his master suite had been but it was doable for now. More of their time than not was spent on the job anyway.

She hesitated as one huge question occurred to her. Who would take care of this child while they worked? Who would make sure he or she was safe and not dropped off on some street corner by some whacked out nanny? Jess had seen the things mothers and fathers as well as caregivers could do to children, and still she wanted to believe that most would never harm them.

Was the woman in the dark glasses really the child's mother? Why, nine hours later, had no one reported the little blonde girl missing?

*Clear your mind.* More than ever before, she needed to learn to relax at least for a few hours each evening. Her health had to be top priority.

She was home. The too small, over an old garage apartment made Jess happy. Even with the BPD cruiser that had pulled into the spot Hayes had vacated serving as a watchdog.

She exhaled a lungful of tension and felt her lips stretch into her first real smile of the day. "Sorry I'm late."

At the bottom of the stairs, Dan leaned down and left a kiss on her cheek. "You're right on time." He looked beyond her and waved. "Turn and wave to your landlord."

Jess twisted at the waist and gave a wave to George.

"That is one creepy old guy," Dan muttered.

"He's eccentric," Jess argued as she led the way up the stairs.

"If you say so."

Inside the spicy smell of garlic and tomato sauce had her stomach rumbling. "You cooked?"

"Spaghetti and garlic bread with a nice salad." He closed and locked the door then armed the security system.

"Smells great!" She dropped her bag by the sofa. "You go ahead before it gets cold. I need a shower." She stared down at the bloodstain on her jacket. She loved this suit but there would be no getting that out.

Dan nodded. "I heard. You okay?"

Jess thought about that for a second. She'd told people all day that she was fine, why change her tune now? "Yes." She lifted her chin resolutely. "Tired and hungry, that's all."

"Get in the shower." He ushered her in the direction of the bathroom door. "I'll round up something comfortable for you to slip into."

"Thanks." Before she moved, she stood there a moment to admire the man she loved with all her heart. He'd shed the business suit and donned jeans and a polo that made him look exactly like one of those guys on the cover of GQ. Except better. What she loved more than the casually sexy clothes was his bare feet. To Jess his feet were the epitome of sexy. And those dimples. She glanced up at the man watching her as intently as she was watching him. She had always loved those dimples.

"Go," he ordered, "before you start something that can't wait until after dinner."

Jess laughed as she kicked off her shoes. It was good to be home. *With Dan.*

Not bothering to close the door, she turned on the spray of water and then stripped off her clothes. She spent the obligatory minute scrutinizing her face and the new lines she always found. By the time she climbed into the old claw foot tub with its wraparound shower curtain, the water was nice and warm. For a minute, she stood beneath the spray and soaked up the warmth. It was so much easier to block the ugliness when she closed her eyes and let the fluid heat flow around her. Her stomach wasn't going to be satisfied so easily, it growled a reminder. Using her favorite body wash, she scrubbed her skin to rid herself of the unpleasant images, sounds, and smells she had absorbed today. She scrubbed her forehead until it was a miracle she had any skin left there. The idea that Spears's blood had no doubt penetrated into her pores made her want to rip off that part of her face.

When the water started to cool, she shut off the valves. She couldn't wait to eat. If she didn't know better she would swear she hadn't eaten all day. Strange thing was, for most of her life she had been one of those people who forgot to eat half the time. Not anymore. She was ravenous all the time.

Dan had left her sweat pants and a tee on the closed toilet lid. She smiled at the slinky panties he'd added to the pile. Pink and lacy. Those definitely were not comfortable. But if he liked them she could deal with a little discomfort. Having a man who cooked was worth a little aggravation. A quick slathering of lotion and moisturizer and she was good to go.

He'd already heaped salad onto a plate for her when she came out of the bathroom feeling tremendously better than she'd felt going in. "This looks great." A glass of wine would be so nice.

Dan grinned. "I know what you're thinking."

She hoped not. Made her sound like a lush. She'd been thinking about alcohol since leaving that interview room this afternoon. "I doubt it." She pulled out her chair and collapsed. Her feet were aching from the same kind of heels she'd always worn. What was it about pregnancy that had a woman's body rebelling so? Her clothes didn't fit and her I-refuse-to-wear-cop-shoes Mary Janes were killing her lately.

Still grinning, Dan grabbed a bottle from the fridge. "I picked it up on the way home."

Jess frowned. Wine? "I can't have alcohol."

"It's alcohol free." He deftly uncorked the bottle and poured a robust serving in both their stemmed glasses. "I did a little research on line. It's safe for expectant mothers."

Oh Lord. Was she ready to be a mother? She'd managed to come to terms with the reality that she was pregnant—that a child was coming in seven or so months whether she was ready or not. Somehow using the term mother seemed far more overwhelming.

"That was nice of you." She really, really had to talk to Lil. She had so many questions and needed her sister's input.

Dan set the bottle aside and reached for his glass. He gave the not actually wine a taste and made a face that wasn't exactly agreeable. "Not too bad."

Which meant it was probably perfectly awful. Jess risked a sip. Maybe he was right. "It's fair."

He joined her at the table. "Cheers." He held his glass out. She tapped it with her own and echoed his sentiment.

"Do you think this Bellamy character was repeating what he'd heard on the news or on the streets?"

Jess had to chew for a second before she could answer. She was so hungry. When she swallowed, she made a satisfied sound. "This is so good."

Dan laughed. "Why don't you eat and we'll talk about the day afterward?"

Jess didn't argue. She dug in, finishing every morsel on her plate before abandoning her fork. She enjoyed a little more of the alcohol free wine while Dan finished his meal. He hadn't wolfed his dinner down like a starving dog as she had.

She would be enormous before this was over. If she'd stayed in better shape before this would be so much easier. But how was someone who worked the hours she did supposed to find time for a run or any other kind of workout?

When Dan looked at her expectantly, she remembered his question. "Terry Bellamy recited that same Bible verse the Vance sisters used." Jess shrugged, suddenly tired. "He couldn't have known unless Spears or one of his followers told him."

That news darkened Dan's expression. "I don't care what Gant says, I think Spears is right here in Birmingham."

Jess wished she could debate his conclusion, but she was relatively certain he was correct. "He has to be."

"You look like you need a nice neck rub?"

Well that was an abrupt change of subject, albeit a welcome one.

"You're tired. You've had one hell of a day," he explained a little too hastily.

Wait just a minute here. Jess's gaze narrowed. "What's going on? What is it you're not looking forward to telling me?"

He stood and reached for her hand. "Come on. Let's get comfortable. I'll clean this up later."

"I'll clean up. You cooked. Isn't that the way it's done?" She stood and reached for her plate. The quickest way to get the truth was to pretend she didn't care.

"Come on." He took her hand in his and tugged her toward the sofa. "I do have something to talk to you about."

She eyed him speculatively. "If you told your mother, I'm going to be seriously pissed."

He settled on the sofa and pulled her down next to him. "We will tell my family together as we planned."

"Okay, so what is it you need to tell me?" She hoped it wasn't more bad news. She couldn't handle anymore *bad* tonight.

"I hired an attorney."

Jess frowned in confusion and then it hit her. "You're worried."

"No, I'm being cautious. I'm not waiting until they make a move. I have too much to protect." His left arm went around her shoulders while his right hand rested against her belly. "Whatever's going on, I'm not going to be caught with my pants down."

The image his words evoked made her laugh. "I'm sorry," she offered. "Nothing about this is even remotely funny, but I think if I don't laugh I might just cry. You don't want to get caught with your pants down and I'm wondering how in the world I'll handle tutus and dance lessons. I've never had a dance lesson in my life!"

He was the one laughing then. "It's not too late to take a dance class." He kissed her cheek. "I wouldn't mind seeing you in a tutu."

"Seriously, how are we going to do this?" She searched his eyes, wishing she could feel the confidence she saw there. "What if I forget something important?" She opted not to mention her worries about forgetting to pick up their child after school or practice of one sort or another.

"We'll manage," he promised. "You'll see."

She hoped he was right. "So, do I know this attorney you hired?"

"I don't think so." He tucked a stray strand of hair behind her ear. "We attended Brighton together. Frank Teller."

Well that said it all. The legal eagle was a fellow alumnus of Dan's. He would surely see that Dan was covered. "Is he good?"

"The best defense attorney in the state."

She nodded her approval. "I'm glad. We have to attack this problem from all angles since it's determined not to go away."

He kissed her forehead. "I won't let this tear us apart." He tucked a finger under her chin and lifted her gaze to his. "You have my word."

She couldn't tell him but she intended to do the same. One way or another she would get to the bottom of this.

"Have you decided on a doctor? You shouldn't keep putting off that appointment."

She'd only found out she was pregnant eight days ago, but the point was a valid one. "I did some research and made an appointment for tomorrow. If I like her I'll stick with her."

"Her?"

"Anita Fortune. She's about our age and has a great website. If she's half as good as the reviews I found on some of the physician rating sites, I'll be more than satisfied."

"When is the appointment? I should come," Dan offered.

Jess didn't want to leave him out, but she preferred to do this with as little fanfare as possible. "One of the reasons I chose her is because she's at the UAB Women & Infants Center. It won't be as obvious why I'm there. If Spears is watching, I don't want him to find out about the baby."

Dan's expression turned somber. "Good point."

"I'm sorry." She snuggled close to him. "I wish you were coming."

"There'll be plenty more appointments." His arm tightened around her. "Who's taking you?"

"Hayes."

"Good. Okay." Dan played with her damp hair. "So when do you want to tell the folks?"

Jess resisted the urge to cringe. "Not that I'm putting off telling them, but can we do that later in the week? I'd like to get this appointment out of the way and I need to talk to Lil. I have to tell her first, Dan." There was still the test for Wilson's disease. Since Lil's diagnosis, Jess had been meaning to go for the test. Lil's children had tested negatively. Jess was hoping for the same. The disease was hereditary and completely controllable, but who wanted any disease?

"You should tell Lil first." He smiled. "I wish I could be there to see the look on her face. She is going to be so happy."

They were supposed to have told their families over the weekend but the latest abduction by Spears had nixed their plans. "She'll be the best aunt any child could ever want. And you'll be the best father." Jess reached up and kissed him on the lips.

"We should start thinking about names," he said between kisses.

"We should," she agreed as she deepened the kiss.

When they both needed to catch their breath, Dan murmured against her lips, "You're not too tired?"

She'd been more exhausted than usual lately, but somehow she wasn't feeling so tired at the moment. "Not *that* tired."

Dan scooped her into his arms and moved to the bed. He placed her gently there. "I hope you're wearing those sexy little pink panties."

"What else would I be wearing?" She reached for the hem of her tee.

The buzz of the sensors on the stairs warned someone was headed up to their door.

Dan threw up his arms. "Oh come on!" He scooted off the bed and stamped to the door as a firm knock sounded against it. After a view through the security peephole, he turned back to Jess. "It's George."

"He probably has mail for me." As annoying as he could be, she felt sorry for the old man. He seemed so lonely. She got up, straightened her clothes, and tried smoothing the curls her hair was drying into—an impossible task. Giving up, she hurried to the door. The sooner she found out what he wanted, the sooner they could get back to couple time.

She disarmed the alarm and flipped all the locks. With a big smile in place, she opened the door. "George, hello. Do I have some mail?" She'd had a few pieces show up in his mailbox. She wasn't actually expecting anything. The utilities were included in the rent. He'd had cable and Internet installed for her and included those as well. Anything important came to the office.

Across the room, plates clacked together loudly enough to have cracked the stoneware. Dan was not a happy camper. She'd have to make this up to him.

George pulled his hand from behind his back and produced a perfect bouquet of red and pink roses. "I thought these might brighten your day."

"Thank you! They're beautiful." She accepted the bundle of thorny roses, careful not to get pricked. George Louis was a talented gardener. He had flowerbeds and shrubs all over the place.

"The heat has taken a toll on the roses, I'm afraid. Those are probably the last truly remarkable ones of the season."

She inhaled the pleasant scent. "They really are gorgeous. Let me find something to put them in. Come on in."

In the kitchen, more of the clacking sounded.

"Have you had dinner, George?" Since she was at the sink looking for a pitcher or something big enough for the flowers, Dan shot her a sour look. She grinned.

"Oh, I've already eaten." George stood at the door like a newly trained soldier feeling ill at ease in the company of the top brass. "I like to get dinner out of the way by six. My sister didn't like eating later in the evening so I guess I developed her habit."

His sister had been dead for years. One of these days, Jess was going to get the story on George Louis and his sister. The two had, from what she'd been told, lived in that big house of his for years before she passed away. He'd taken care of her. Multiple sclerosis, if Jess recalled correctly.

Jess set the pitcher filled with water and flowers on the table Dan had cleared. "Thank you so much, George. They are really beautiful."

George smiled so big his cheeks nudged his glasses a little higher up the bridge of his nose. "I'm glad you like them." He adjusted his glasses, gave Jess a nod as he shuffled his feet. "I should go. Have a nice evening."

Jess thanked him again and locked the door behind him. When the security system was armed once more, she rested her attention on the man scouring dishes. That was another thing this place didn't have—a dishwasher.

She moved up behind him and looped her arms around his waist. "I'm still not tired."

He shut off the water, dried his hands, and did a one eighty in her arms. "Knowing our luck my mother will show up at the door next."

"I don't think so." She led him to the bed and climbed onto the cool covers. "I think we're safe now."

He dragged off his shirt and reached for his jeans. The scar on his abdomen reminded her how close she'd come to losing him. Her heart ached at the memory. By the time he'd kicked free of the denim, she was breathless with anticipation.

She closed her eyes and let him undress her. She didn't want to think, she just wanted to feel and put one more day haunted by Spears behind her.

Maybe tomorrow he would make a mistake.

# CHAPTER SEVEN

Lori sat hunched over the dining table, her notes spread around her. She had reviewed all that video footage, and then she'd checked every available database for missing children. It was late and she wasn't showing any signs of calling it a day.

Chet threaded his fingers through his hair and wished he could say the right words to make her understand she hadn't done anything wrong. Didn't matter what he said, she wasn't buying it. He checked his cell again. Still nothing from Sherry. Not even a text. His ex-wife had let him talk to his son on Saturday afternoon. Chet had tried his best to figure out their location from the background sounds and every little word Chester said, but he had failed. The kid sounded happy and safe. That was what mattered. Even if Chet wanted to shake Sherry for taking off with their son like that, he had to admit she'd been the smart one.

He wandered over to the window and checked for the BPD cruiser outside. Didn't matter that he and Lori were both cops, they still had a surveillance detail. So did Chief Harris and almost everyone close to her. This Spears thing was way out of control. The FBI had nothing. The bastard could be anywhere—right across the damned street, for that matter.

Nothing would surprise Chet at this point. He went to the kitchen and grabbed a couple of icy cold beers from the fridge. Maybe he could convince Lori to take a break. He set a beer down next to her and pulled out a chair. "You should take five."

She shook her head. "I still have a couple lists to go through a second time."

He unscrewed the top on his beer and set it aside. "You think if you stay focused on work that you won't have to look at me or anyone else." She glanced at him but quickly looked away. "You didn't do anything wrong, Lori. How many ways do I have to say it? The chief has told you. Everyone has told you."

She lifted her gaze to his, those green eyes glinting with anger. "You're wrong and repeating the same bogus statement isn't going to change the facts of what happened."

He rubbed a hand over his face before resting his chin in his palm. "This won't be the last time you make what you feel is the wrong decision. Maybe next time someone will get hurt or worse. You might as well get used to the idea now. It will happen again." She cut him a warning glare. He ignored it.

"The real question is, are you a strong enough cop to take the pressure?"

She slammed her pen down on the table. "That tactic won't work either. I made a mistake, and Jess could have been killed. Those minutes play over and over in my head every time I look at her."

"But she wasn't."

"That's beside the point." Lori ran her fingers through her long hair and then massaged her temples. "It was my job to watch out for her and I screwed up." She glared at him again. "I should have let Clint go with her. He wanted to and I blew him off because I was jealous of how he joined the team—after I recommended him—and tried to take over. I," she poked herself in the chest with her thumb, "made the wrong choice. Nothing anyone says is going to change that."

Chet set his beer down with a plop. This was enough. "All right. You screwed up, Detective. You took your eyes off that bathroom door for a minute, and those two freaks got in. The chief could have been killed. You made a mistake. Two actually. You operated on emotion and you let yourself be distracted." He shrugged casually no matter that his gut was clenched in a thousand knots. "Get over it."

She stared at him, her jaw slack with shock. "I only looked away for a few seconds. Chief Black burst in shouting like some television drama cop and I… looked away. Five, ten seconds tops."

Chet nodded. "You did what any other human would have done. I would have done it and Hayes would have done it."

Tears spilled past her lashes. "But you didn't do it. Hayes didn't do it. I did."

Chet fell to his knees next to her chair. "Baby, I wish I could make that awful feeling go away, but only time will do that." She burrowed her face into his shoulder and sobbed. He put his arms around her and held on tight. "You are a damned good cop. Don't let this one thing shake your confidence. If you do, you'll second guess every decision you make from now on. Let it go, baby. Let it go."

She fisted her fingers in his shirt. "I can't." She lifted her face to his. "I was too cocky. I see that now. I'd never made a mistake like that and I thought I was above it." She swiped at her nose with the back of her hand. "I was wrong, Chet. I'm not as good as I thought."

He took her face in his hands and made her look at him. "Don't let him do this to you. Spears has already won too many rounds. Don't let him win this one too. You're stronger than that. The chief needs you backing her up. She's counting on us now more than ever."

"I thought I was strong."

He smoothed the dampness away from her cheeks with the pads of his thumbs. "Show me what you've found on the little girl. I'm really worried about her."

As Lori brushed away the last of her tears, Chet drew his chair next to hers. Maybe if they focused on the case together, she would put last Friday's event out of her mind for a while.

"She's about the same age as Chester, wouldn't you say?" Chet offered.

Lori nodded. "That's what I'm thinking. The pediatrician who examined her estimated four years. But she's so small."

"She is." He picked up the photo of the child. "Did you notice how much she looks like the chief?"

"The blond hair and the brown eyes." Lori nodded. "Yeah, it's a little creepy." She studied Chet then. "Do you think Jess thought about that? I mean, they don't share any facial features really but the coloring is so similar."

"I'm sure she considered that Spears had picked the little girl because she has blond hair and brown eyes. That has to be really freaking her out." He grabbed his beer and downed a satisfying gulp. "It's bad enough when an adult is missing or murdered, but it's hell when it's a kid."

Lori put her arms around his neck and pressed her forehead to his cheek. "I'm sorry. I've been feeling so sorry for myself I didn't stop to think how this business with Chester must be hurting you." She searched his eyes. "You know Sherry made a smart move, right?"

He nodded, albeit reluctantly. "Yeah. I should have been the one to suggest the move. I was too busy being a cop to notice my own child was in danger."

"I see how it is." Lori took his face in her hands and made him look her in the eye as he had done to her a moment ago. "Now who's blaming himself for something he couldn't possibly have foreseen?" She let him go, leaned back in her chair, and crossed her arms over her chest. "It's okay for you to feel bad because you aren't perfect but not me? Ha!"

He held his hands up in surrender. "Okay, okay. We both need to cut ourselves some slack."

"Maybe," she suggested, "we need a long soak in our nice garden tub before climbing into that comfy bed we haven't made love in for the past two nights."

He lifted her onto his lap and decided this was a good time to tell her his news. "I had a break today while you and Cook were reviewing video footage and Hayes was off with the chief interviewing that crazy homeless dude."

Lori shuddered. "He tried to reenact what Matthew Reed did to that FBI agent."

"Sounds like," Chet agreed.

Lori had been abducted by Spears's deceased protégé, Matthew Reed. He'd held her for days, tormented her relentlessly, including making her watch as he tortured two other women, one didn't survive. Lori almost died as well. The bastard had used her greatest fear against her—the fear of drowning. Spears loved using his victims' fears to torture them. Chet hoped he got just five minutes alone with the guy before he went to hell.

"What did you do during this break?" she asked, curious.

He'd been waiting for the right moment to share this news with her. Might as well be now. "I made the appointment for the surgery. Two weeks from today."

Lori's face lit up. "He thinks it can be done?"

Chet nodded. "He does. Since it's only been three years, he says there's a very high chance of success. I'll be off work for a few days, but as soon as he gives the go ahead we can start trying to make a baby."

Lori stilled. "You want to start right away?"

Chet held his breath. Hoped this wasn't going to be a sticking point. "Sometimes scar tissues forms and closes things up again. The surgeon says it's important that we try right away. The first year is crucial."

"Wow." Lori looked away. "I'm not sure how I feel about that schedule."

He didn't want to rush her, but she needed to understand the hurdles they were facing. Sherry had insisted on the vasectomy after Chester was born, and Chet had done what he hoped would save his marriage. But it hadn't. He prayed that desperate decision wasn't going to cost him the woman he loved now.

"We don't have to if you're not ready," he assured her. "I can put the surgery off. The problem is, the longer I wait before I get it reversed the lower the odds of success."

"I didn't realize we'd be up against a timeline."

"I'm sorry," he offered. The words echoed impotently around them.

She got up, leaving the warm place she'd made in his lap. "I'm beat. Maybe I'll just shower and hit the sack."

Chet reached for his beer. So much for lightening the mood with what he thought was good news.

# CHAPTER EIGHT

Amanda Brownfield drew in a lungful of smoke and held it for as long as she could before exhaling into the night. "Mmm." There was just about nothing on God's green earth tasted as good as a cigarette after sex.

The ground shifted beneath her with his twisting and squirming around. "Be still," she screamed! She worked harder at staying put, digging in her heels and pressing her butt harder into the dirt. She thought about using the Taser again but she was pretty sure it wasn't gonna be necessary.

He was just about done.

Weatherman was calling for rain tomorrow. The dirt would pack down all nice and neat then. She stared at the bright glow of cherry at the end of her cigarette. She could toss this thing into all the dry underbrush and burn this whole place down once and for all.

What did she need with this hellhole now anyway? She had bigger plans.

The ground beneath her stopped moving.

She smiled. "Good boy," she murmured. "You just go right on to hell where you belong." She dragged in another deep draw from her smoke. Oh yeah, there was just about nothing else that tasted as good as a cigarette after sex.

Except maybe having one after killing a no good son of a bitch like the one she'd killed tonight.

Amanda laughed as she wiggled her bottom against the loose dirt. She'd forgotten how much fun this could be.

# CHAPTER NINE

Jess waited in the examining room for Dr. Fortune to return. The labs were out of the way and the exam was over. The requisite paper gown was properly disposed of and she felt comfortable again in her red suit. Her life was so out of control that it felt good to wear a power color. Especially today. There was no more pretending this wasn't real.

Her life was never going to be the same. She'd survived starting over in her career and moving back home after more than two decades. No reason she couldn't handle parenthood.

Moments from now the doctor would waltz in for the doctor-patient pep talk. Jess's bag was full of pamphlets and a prescription for, as well as a sample pack of, prenatal vitamins. She was good to go.

Except her head was spinning. She had flipped through the pamphlets for the first few minutes of her wait, one of which showed the stages of development in pregnancy. She shouldn't have looked.

If she'd been worried before about taking care of herself for the baby's benefit, she was outright terrified now.

Okay, moment of truth—how did anyone in her right mind do this? There was so much evil out there. So much uncertainty. Giving herself credit, it wasn't as if she'd planned to get pregnant. One or two missed pills had set the stage.

Forty-two and she'd made a sophomoric mistake. She was far too old to accidentally get pregnant. Jess closed her eyes and heaved a sigh. Her sister was going to be over the moon as soon as she had a nice long laugh over how Jess came to be with child. Children had not been on her ten-year-plan much less next year's calendar. She wasn't even married or engaged—well, not technically. Dan had made it clear he wanted to get married, but there hadn't been a proposal or ring.

Jess sighed. How had her life grown so complicated in a mere six weeks? Before returning to Birmingham, work had been her life. She hadn't needed anything else to fulfill her. Who needed the white picket fence and kids? She'd had a stellar career with the Bureau—okay so maybe she'd blown her *stellar* record a week or two before coming home. She'd had the respect of every agent with whom she'd ever worked until that last week or two. Prior to that, she'd had nothing to worry about but catching the bad guy—the solitary goal had defined her.

On some level, she couldn't deny that coming home had made her see what she had given up...

what she was missing. Whether by subconscious design or dumb mistake, here she was with diapers and childcare and doctor visits in her future. Her eyes went wide. They needed a new house. The apartment was fine for the two of them, but it wasn't going to work after this child was born.

Would Dan want to build in his old neighborhood? Jess would never in a million years fit in with the Brookies of Mountain Brook. She would always be the girl from the other side of the tracks. Well, she had made friends with Sylvia and Gina. It wasn't that anyone else had the ability to make Jess feel inferior. Her accomplishments spoke for themselves. The problem was some people would always see her as an outsider as Katherine Burnett did. Would that change when she became a Burnett too?

Jess sagged with the weight of it all. Friends and neighborhoods were the least of her concerns. Two women were missing, Rory Stinnett and Monica Atmore. Victims of the sociopath obsessed with Jess. Dan had become one of his primary targets. And she was his ultimate target no matter that, for now, Spears appeared to be content playing with her.

How did she protect the child she carried? Or the people she loved?

Thankfully, the doctor showed up at that moment. Good thing, otherwise Jess might have worried herself into a panic attack.

Dr. Fortune smiled. "You've been reviewing the pamphlets."

Jess frowned. She'd already stuffed them all back into her bag. "How did you know?"

"The look of panic on your face is one I've seen many times." The doctor settled on the stool next to the small wall mounted desk and considered the tablet she carried. She tapped a few keys. "It'll be a few days before all your labs are back. I'm not so concerned about the Wilson's disease since you don't have any symptoms. We'll know soon enough if there's anything to worry about there." She typed a note into Jess's record.

Her sister had recently been diagnosed with Wilson's disease after some scary symptoms. Thank goodness, they caught it in time to reverse the damage and get her on the right track. The disease had caused her body to not properly metabolize copper. The subsequent build up wreaked havoc on her organs.

"Is there a due date I should put on my calendar?" Jess ventured, her pulse fluttering like hummingbird wings.

The doctor laughed. "There are a lot of dates you should put on your calendar, but based on your last menstrual cycle, we've calculated your due date as April twentieth. A little later we'll do an ultrasound that'll confirm that date one way or the other."

*April twentieth.* Jess had about seven months and three weeks to get prepared for motherhood. Goose bumps tumbled over her skin. *Not nearly long enough!*

"You may continue to have the same bouts of the nausea you've been experiencing for a few more weeks. Generally, when you reach the second trimester that subsides."

Second trimester. Okay. "Is there anything I should be concerned about moving forward?"

Dr. Fortune closed the record. "We'll put you on the routine pregnancy schedule and I'll see you again next month. Take your vitamins, keep a healthy diet, and get plenty of rest. Your body is working extra hard right now, it needs sufficient down time. There are a few more tests we'll want to do a little later related to your age, otherwise, that's it."

Her age. She was old. Jess wilted a little bit more. "Thank you, Doctor."

Fortune paused at the door. "I meant to ask, is the handsome gentleman outside the father? He could've come in with you, you know."

Jess didn't need a mirror to know that red had rushed up her cheeks and all the way to the roots of her hair. "No. No. He's a detective on my team." No need to go into all her other troubles with her obstetrician. "My... the father couldn't get away from work." She chewed her lip. That excuse made Dan sound as if he didn't care so she quickly added, "He'll be here next time."

The doctor gave a nod. "See you in a month."

Jess didn't move for a minute after the doctor had gone. When she'd awoke this morning, she wondered whether this baby would be a boy or a girl and if he or she would have blond hair and brown eyes like the little girl left on the street yesterday.

Maybe she would drop by and check on the child. Make sure she was okay. It would give her something to do besides going back to the office before meeting Lil for lunch. Jess stood, smoothed her skirt, and walked to the door. She hesitated, her hand on the lever. In her entire adult life, this was the first time she'd ever wanted to do anything else more than she wanted to go to work.

Not a good sign.

REDMONT ROAD, 11:20 A.M.

The home was a nice one in a very good neighborhood. The lieutenant followed Jess up the sidewalk. Mrs. Wettermark had called ahead and informed the family that Jess would be stopping by to see the little girl. Wettermark had insisted the child was fine, but Jess would feel more comfortable when she saw for herself. It was foolish really. If the case investigator said she was fine, then Jess should accept her word. Somehow, she couldn't.

She pressed the doorbell, listened for the chime, and then waited. Inside a dog barked. Judging by the deep boom it was a larger one. She supposed it was nice for kids to be around pets.

Was that something else she would need to pencil into her life?

Sheesh. To be so small, kids came with seemingly endless requirements.

She glanced back to the street and noted the BPD cruiser waiting patiently for her next move.

"You were on the news again this morning."

Jess glanced at the detective standing next to her. "I'm thrilled."

Hayes chuckled. "According to the reporter, the station's getting tons of mail in support of you. They're calling you a city treasure."

A laugh burst from her lips. "If that's the case, I am woefully under paid."

He grinned. "You aren't the only one. The whole team should be getting hazard pay for protecting a city treasure."

"Need I remind you that this treasure is perfectly capable of—?"

"Taking care of herself," he finished for her.

"Don't you forget it either, Lieutenant." Jess held her head high and her shoulders back. Being pregnant didn't mean she wasn't capable of doing exactly what she'd always done—for now anyway.

The door opened and a woman with one kid on her hip and two more clinging to her legs filled the space. Growling, a big black Lab poked his head between her and the door.

"Quiet, Samson!" the woman ordered. The big Lab dropped his head and backed away. The woman looked from Jess to Hayes and back, then smiled as if she were the happiest woman on earth.

Jess couldn't see how that was possible by any stretch of the imagination. She flashed her badge. "I'm Deputy Chief Harris."

"Karen Graham." She backed up to open the door wider, the children and the dog moved in time with her as if the steps were a carefully choreo-graphed routine. "We've been expecting you. Mrs. Wettermark sent me your photo."

Jess appreciated Wettermark's quick work. She'd expected to have to wait outside until Mrs. Graham confirmed Jess was who she said she was.

"Thank you." Jess followed her inside. Hayes closed the door and caught up. The interior of the house was just as nice as the exterior. "You have a lovely home."

"Thank you. We bought the house for the kids."

Jess hoped she had erased the frown that had formed on her forehead before the woman noticed. "How many children do you have?"

"Since we couldn't have any of our own," Karen smiled at the toddler in her arms, "we decided to buy a house big enough for all the ones who needed a family and didn't have one." She turned that smile toward Jess. "We take care of the children until a permanent home is found or they're returned to their parents, so there's always lots of coming and going around here."

"That's an enormous sacrifice." Jess glanced into the family room to her right where three more chil-dren played.

"It is," Karen agreed, "but we love it. Would you like to see her now?"

Jess nodded. "I would."

Karen ushered the children tagging along with her into the family room with the others. Then she led the way to the dining room. "She doesn't feel comfortable with the other children yet so I'm letting her draw at the table."

"Why don't you wait here, Lieutenant?" No need to overwhelm the child with another stranger.

"I'll check in with Detective Wells. Give her our location."

Jess left him to it and followed Karen into the dining room. The enormous table seated twelve. Jess was fairly certain she'd never seen a table this large in anyone's home. The Grahams had gone all out.

The little girl sat in one of the big oak chairs, her attention on a length of drawing paper draped over the end of the table. A pile of crayons next to her, she continued to draw without even glancing up.

Jess walked over to the table. When the little girl still didn't look up, she said, "Remember me?"

The little girl looked up then and, incredibly, she smiled. It wasn't much of one but a smile nonetheless. Jess pulled up a chair next to her. "That's a very pretty picture. Is that you?" She pointed to the smaller of the two stick figures.

The little girl nodded.

Jess indicated the larger figure. "Is that your mommy?"

The child shook her head and then she pointed to Jess.

Surprised, Jess gestured to the figure again. "That's me?"

The little girl nodded.

"You see this big thing." Jess set her black bag on the floor. "I take it everywhere." She pointed to the drawing. "If that's me, I need my bag."

The little girl picked up a black crayon and drew a square, that wasn't exactly square, next to the larger stick figure. She looked up at Jess for approval.

Jess took the crayon from her soft little fingers and drew a strap on the box. "There." She placed the crayon back in the pile. "That's perfect."

The little girl scooted off her seat and hugged Jess. Jess wasn't sure what to say or do but her heart did a little dancing around. When the girl held on tight, Jess hugged her back. Tears welled up in her eyes. She'd certainly been hugged by children before. Her sister's kids and... well, she couldn't think of any others at the moment, but she was certain there were more. Her emotional reaction was silly. It took a moment but Jess pulled herself together.

"You know something?" When the little girl looked up at her, Jess smoothed her long blond hair back from her face. "I sure wish I knew your name."

The child curled her finger for Jess to lean closer. Jess lowered her head until her ear was close to the little girl's face. She whispered so softly, Jess barely heard her. She straightened and thrust out her hand. "Nice to meet you, Maddie."

Maddie shook her hand.

"My name is Jess Harris. Do you have another name?"

The little girl shrugged and climbed back onto her chair. She picked up a yellow color and drew a big, round ball above the stick figures. Jess watched her for a few more minutes as she colored the ball yellow. She was going to be late for her lunch with Lil. Feeling a little torn, she said her goodbyes and made her way back into the entry hall where Hayes waited.

At the door, Karen said, "That's the first word she's spoken. At least now we have a name for her."

"I'll let Mrs. Wettermark know," Jess assured her.

As she and Hayes climbed into his car, Jess wondered why Maddie would include Jess in her drawing. The sudden attachment to an adult she'd never met before was odd to say the least... unless she'd been tutored.

What was Spears up to?

With monumental effort, she set those concerns aside. A few minutes of mental preparation were in order. She was about to give her sister some startling news. Calm and collected was essential.

LAKEFRONT TRAIL.
BESSEMER. 1:25 P.M.

Lil passed Jess a cup of coffee. "I'm glad you enjoyed the lasagna. It was my first time making it with vegetables instead of meat." She frowned. "Blake's cholesterol is running a little high. We're getting to that age, you know. Where everything starts to fall apart."

Jess sipped her coffee. "Mmm-hmm." Her sister was not making this easy. They'd made it through lunch. Lil had insisted Hayes join them, which was only right, but it didn't help with setting the stage for Jess to deliver her big news. To his credit, after declining coffee, Hayes had moved into the living room to check in with the office. The day was more than half over and Jess was seriously behind.

She needed to get the news out and be done with it.

Jess set her cup aside. Her hand shook. *Steady, girl.*

"I know what you're going to say," Lil said before Jess could get the words out.

Jess blinked. *How could she possibly know?*

"Yes," Lil declared. "I am cooperating fully with my surveillance detail. I make sure he's out there before I go to bed at night and I look for him first thing in the morning. I don't go anywhere without making sure he's right behind me. I make lemonade, sandwiches, and coffee for him every day. So there, you proud of me?"

The blood pulsing at her temples had Jess half expecting her head to explode with the mounting tension. "Very proud. I want you safe, Lil. I need you." Jess's voice quavered on the last. She cleared her throat. "Anyway, I have some health news too."

"Did you have the test for Wilson's disease? Was it negative? Are you okay?" Lil put her coffee aside and grabbed Jess's hands. "Please tell me you're okay."

"I took the test," Jess assured her. "I'll know in a few days but the doctor was optimistic. I don't have any symptoms of the disease."

Lil blew out a big breath and clasped her cheeks with both hands. "Thank God. You had me worried there for a minute."

*Just tell her.* Jess took a breath. God, oh God. This was going to forever change every single thing. Once the words were out of her mouth, there would be no taking them back. Last week, as crazy as the news had made her, it had been so much easier because no one except Hayes had known—at least not until she told Dan. Once everyone knew, they would all look at her differently. She didn't want to be treated as if she were made of glass.

"You said you had news," Lil prompted. "What news?"

"Well," Jess began. Her foot started to tap against the shiny hardwood of her sister's dining room floor. Jess crossed her legs to stop it. "I... I'm pregnant."

Lil stared at her for a full five seconds, then she burst into laughter. "Good grief, Jess," she said between gasps for air. "I thought you were going to tell me you had cancer or something." She slapped Jess on the shoulder. "It's not April first so stop fooling around."

Lil either didn't believe Jess or she was in shock. "As it turns out, April is when the baby's due." *April Fool.*

Lil stared at her again. She blinked, once, twice. "You're telling me that you're *pregnant?*"

"Yes." Jess nodded just in case the word wasn't penetrating the shock her sister was apparently experiencing. "I went to the doctor this morning for confirmation. I have the prenatal vitamins and the morning sickness. The whole kit and caboodle."

Lil shook her head. "Really, I… don't know what to say." She stood abruptly, grabbed their coffee cups, and headed for the kitchen.

What in the world? Jess followed her sister. This was not at all the reaction she'd expected. Where were the hugs and shouts for joy? The congratulations? "You could say something, Lil."

"There's a lot more to being pregnant than prenatal vitamins," Lil scolded as she placed coffee cups into the dishwasher. "There are all sorts of preparations." She closed the dishwasher and turned to Jess. Her expression shifted to confusion and she shook her head. "Let me get this straight. You want me to believe this is not a joke. You really are pregnant?"

Jess nodded.

Lil's lips trembled. "Oh my God." Tears flowed down her cheeks. "I can't believe it." She shrugged. "I'd hoped and prayed but I never thought it would happen."

Jess wasn't sure what to do. She'd never seen her sister react this way.

"I'll bet Dan is thrilled." Lil hugged her arms around her waist, tears shining on her cheeks. "He's waited all this time. He waited for *you*."

"Dammit, Lil. Now you've made me cry." Jess swiped at the tears. Tried to blink them back.

DEBRA WEBB

"Pregnant women are very emotional," Lil said with a knowing nod.

Jess gave a little shrug. "I know."

Lil suddenly frowned. "My sister is going to have a baby."

Before Jess could open her mouth to reply, Lil threw her arms around Jess and hugged her as if they hadn't seen each other in years. Jess lost her battle with her emotions then. They cried and hugged some more. Jess lost count of the number of times they said I-love-you before they pulled themselves together.

Finally, when they both looked a mess and felt giddy with excitement, they started to laugh. Lil found her voice first. "I'm so proud of you. You're going to be the best mother."

Those were exactly the words Jess had needed to hear.

They got in one more hug before Hayes appeared in the doorway. "We just got a call from the Jackson County Sheriff's department. They have a body. It's Maddie's grandmother."

Jess wished the celebration could have gone on a little while longer, but she had to go back to work. There was a little girl counting on her.

And a murder victim who needed her to find a killer.

# CHAPTER TEN

The old farmhouse was not in Scottsboro proper. It stood well outside town, where cows grazed in pastures and corn and cotton fields dotted the landscape.

Jess got out of the car and studied the one-story house. They'd had to park a good fifty yards from the driveway. Cop cars, along with a fire and rescue truck, lined the narrow driveway from the paved road all the way up to the house. Jess had no desire to be blocked in. Parking on the side of the road suited her just fine. The BPD cruiser that followed her around parked nearby.

Harper's SUV nosed into the open space between the cruiser and Hayes's car. Jess was glad to see two more members of her team. This was well out of their jurisdiction, but the Jackson County sheriff had agreed to sit tight until their arrival. Since there was a link to an ongoing case in Birmingham, and possibly to the Spears investigation, Jess appreciated the sheriff's cooperation. Someone from the

Birmingham Bureau Field Office would be showing up as well but Jess wasn't waiting.

"This is what I call the sticks," Lori said as she joined Jess on the roadside. She looked around. "Hear that?"

Jess certainly did. "Birds and the wind in the trees."

Lori shuddered visibly. "This is way too quiet for me."

It was good to see her acting more like herself. Jess was grateful for any improvement. Maybe this was going to be a good day for moving forward. She'd made a few strides of her own. Her sister had already sent her two text messages about tentative baby shower dates. Lil was in her element. Next, her sister would be planning a wedding for Jess and Dan.

"Reminds me of when we were working the Man in the Moon case," Jess noted. She and Lori had seen some quiet ruralscapes during that investigation. Maybe not this far out in the boonies but similar.

"Let's just hope the locals are as friendly," Lori agreed.

"I think I hear dueling banjos," Harper said as he clipped his shield onto his belt.

"You watch my back," Hayes suggested, "and I'll watch yours."

"Get your game faces on," Jess warned. "We're the interlopers. We need to make a good impression from the start. Small town cops don't appreciate big city cops taking over, or their attitudes."

As they headed for the driveway, Harper gave Hayes and his high-end attire a once over. "We might be in serious trouble already."

Hayes made a dismissive sound. "I guess we'll have to use our charming personalities to make an impression."

Harper shrugged. "Just saying."

At the end of the drive a deputy waited, one hip propped against his cruiser. "You must be the detectives from Birmingham."

Jess didn't miss his pointed look at her shoes. Yes, she loved her high-heeled Mary Jane pumps. So shoot her. She presented her credentials. "I'm Deputy Chief Harris and these are my detectives, Wells, Harper and Hayes. Your sheriff is expecting us."

"Yes, ma'am." He gestured toward the house. "The coroner's on the way. Sheriff called for a forensic unit but it's not here yet either."

"Thank you, Deputy," she glanced at his nametag, "Jones."

He gave one of those nods southern men used for greeting or acknowledgment when they didn't want to bother with words. Hayes charged forward ahead of Jess and Lori while Harper brought up the rear. Between the scattered ruts and the gravel, Jess was confident her heels would never be the same. Oh well. She needed new footwear to go along with the new wardrobe her body would require. Maybe she'd even step it down a little to more practical heels. She grimaced as her shoe heel marred into a soft spot.

*Lots of changes coming.*

With all the shade from the large trees around the house, the yard was more dirt than grass. An old pick-up truck sat under a tree. Didn't look as if it had been moved for a while. A porch ran the length of the front of the home. One end was noticeably lower than the other one. Judging by the rusty metal roof and the peeling clapboard siding, the house was an old one. Beyond the house, there was a barn that looked in even sadder condition. A rusty swing set stood to the left of the house. The image of Maddie swinging there played in Jess's mind. She and Lil had a swing set much like that one when they were kids. Another staple of childhood this baby would need.

Two more uniforms waited on the porch. Neither was the sheriff. Hayes climbed the three steps first.

"Lieutenant Clint Hayes," he said to the deputies. "Chief Harris, Birmingham PD, is here to view the crime scene."

The deputy surveyed the group before turning his attention back to Hayes. "I'll get the sheriff."

Jess joined the lieutenant near the door. "See if we can get one of our guys from forensics out here." For the other deputy's benefit, she added, "Two sets of eyes are always better than one."

"I'll take care of that now," Hayes assured her.

As the detective stepped away, Lori and Harper moved in next to Jess. "Sergeant Harper, I'd like you and the lieutenant to have a look around the property as soon as we've gotten the formalities out of the way. Detective Wells, you and I will go through the steps inside the house."

"Got it," Harper said as he pulled on gloves.

Jess and Lori did the same before pulling on shoe covers. Yet another reason to consider new footwear. These damned shoe covers were not intended for high heels. No doubt the protective wear had been designed by a man. Then again, most female cops didn't share Jess's one vanity—clothes and shoes.

The screen door opened with a creak and a tall man who looked to be about Jess's age joined them on the porch. "Chief Harris, I'm Sheriff Mike Foster." He extended his hand. "It's a pleasure to make your acquaintance, circumstances notwithstanding."

Jess shook the man's hand. "I appreciate your call, Sheriff. We're anxious to find out what's going on here."

"Come on in. We're still waiting for the coroner and the evidence folks."

Jess and Lori followed the sheriff inside. The overhead lights had been turned on although the illumination they provided was minimal, and the curtains had been pushed aside, but the grime on the windows prevented much light from getting through. Rustic wood floors, walls, and ceilings, along with a stone fireplace, continued the old farmhouse design theme to the interior of the home. The pale yellow paint on the walls was in serious need of a fresh coat. A tattered sofa and chair along with a couple of tables were the only furnishings. No television, only an old radio that looked more like a piece of furniture.

"Straight in front of you is the kitchen," the sheriff explained. "Down the hall we got three small bedrooms and one bath. Margaret Brownfield's body is in the bedroom at the end of the hall on the left. Looks like she's been gone for a few hours. We put out a BOLO on her daughter, Amanda. No sign of her or the old clunker she drives."

"Amanda is Maddie's mother?" Jess hoped Amanda wasn't a murderer in addition to a negligent parent.

Sheriff Foster dragged his hat off and smoothed his hair before settling it back into place. "Unfortunately for that little girl, she is. She's got an arrest record that includes drug possession, disorderly conduct, and petty theft. Most folks think she's a little crazy."

"Is there a father in the picture?" Jess was guessing not based on the drawing Maddie had made.

Foster shrugged. "I can't say for sure. There's a boyfriend and he's unaccounted for as well. We checked with his employer but he hasn't been to work in weeks. Name's Brock Clements. He's pretty much a no-good drunk. According to the neighbors, he's been hanging around here for months. We got a BOLO out on him and his old truck, too. It was his momma who found Margaret. She came over here looking for her son since he hadn't been home in a while."

"Two of my detectives are having a look around outside," Jess let the sheriff know. "Detective Wells and I will start in here, if you have no objections."

"Make yourself at home, Chief. My crime scene is your crime scene." The cell on his hip rang. "Excuse me, ladies."

Jess was grateful the house wasn't full of cops, but there was no way to know how many had tracked through when the scene was first discovered. Since none wore gloves or shoe covers and she hadn't noticed any discarded protective wear, she had to assume they'd left prints behind. *Fabulous.*

"You want to start in here?" Lori asked.

Jess nodded. "Then we'll move on to the kitchen."

The victim was dead. They could do nothing for the woman except find out who murdered her. The best way to do that was to understand how she lived and who might have been at odds with her or wanted something she possessed.

Two framed photos of Maddie sat on one of the tables. In one of the photos, she sat in the lap of a thirtyish woman with brown hair. Jess picked up the photo and looked at the woman's nose and mouth. Those were about the only two features they'd been able to see in the video footage of Maddie being dropped off.

"That's the woman who dropped Maddie off," Lori said, voicing the conclusion Jess had reached as well.

Jess passed her the photo. "I'm guessing that's Amanda, her mother."

"I'll check with Sheriff Foster."

While Lori made the ID, Jess moved to piles of newspapers in one corner of the room. Stacks of the local newspaper as well a smaller pile of more recent editions of the Birmingham News. Jess picked up the top copy and noted the headline about the gruesome murders she had investigated last week had been cut from the front page. As she sifted through the piles, the one thing the papers had in common was that any news related to Jess and her investigations in Birmingham or to Spears were missing.

It looked as if she had a fan. Was it the mother or the grandmother?

In the kitchen, the rustic country look continued. A few wall cabinets held dry and canned goods as well as the usual cooking and eating utensils. The fridge hosted a gallon of milk and a block of cheese, both near their expiration dates. A couple of packs of meat were wrapped in butcher paper and stored in the freezer. A stick figure drawing very similar to the one Maddie had drawn today hung on the side of the fridge. A small bag of apples lay on the counter.

There were no indications of forced entry or a struggle in the kitchen or the living room. Nothing appeared out of place. That same quiet she'd noticed outside permeated the inside of the home. Jess couldn't help wondering if the silence was why Maddie didn't like to talk or to be with other children. She was accustomed to quiet.

Lori caught up with Jess in the hall. "The woman in the photo is Amanda, Maddie's mother. She's thirty-eight. Never been married, but according to the sheriff, her list of boyfriends would make the top ten list of Jackson County's repeat offenders. Drugs and assault mostly."

"One mystery solved." Jess could imagine the sort of life Maddie had endured.

The first bedroom on the right was the little girl's. A small bed and dresser along with a few toys and the pink walls made the room a little brighter than the rest of the house. Plain white curtains adorned the single window that looked out over the front yard. Jess picked up the doll lying on the bed. It was the kind with a soft body and painted hair. Its dress was home made.

Jess placed the doll back on the bed and moved on to the next bedroom on the right. This one smelled like incense and was littered with empty beer cans. A narrow bed and dresser were the only furnishings. Lori pushed the curtains to the side of the single window to let in more light. Apparently, the sheriff had taken a quick look in here and decided there wasn't anything to see.

Three of the four walls were the same yellow as the living room and hall, but the wall behind the bed was draped with striped sheets. At the foot of the bed, Jess lifted the sheet from the wall and had a look underneath. Startled, she drew back, let the sheet fall back against the wall.

Lori looked from Jess to the sheet. "What's back there?"

Jess took a deep breath and ordered her pulse to slow. "Let's get those sheets down."

Lori climbed onto the bed and tugged the ends of the sheets loose from the nails holding them. Jess piled them onto the end of the bed.

"Holy shit," Lori muttered.

Taped onto the wall were dozens of photos and newspaper articles about Jess. The photos and articles had been precisely placed in chronological order.

"This one is three years old," Lori said, pointing to one of the articles.

Jess moved closer, her heart picking up its pace. There was one article that went back five years. She wasn't named in the article, but it was about the investigation she had been working on as a profiler for the Bureau. Around that same time the Bureau had labeled a new serial killer—the Player. She had been assigned the case. If only she had known how that one case was going to change her life.

"Wait." Lori looked from the article to Jess. "How could she have known this was about you?"

Jess shook her head. "Maybe she was following news about the Player, and the natural progression was for her to follow me when the story about my screw up hit the news early last month."

Lori moved farther down the wall. She tapped a photo. "When was this taken?"

Jess looked at the photo in question. She was at dinner… with Wesley, her ex-husband. A year ago? "How did she get…?" No need to finish the question. Jess knew exactly where she'd gotten it. That meant just one thing. *Spears.*

"Spears," Lori said, the disbelief in her voice matching that on her face, "he's been watching you for a long time, Jess. He must have given Amanda these photos."

Ice hardened in Jess's veins as the reality spread through her body. She braced against it. The concept that Spears may have latched onto her far longer ago than she realized thundered in her ears. *Don't think about it.* A woman had been murdered in this house. That was where her focus had to be. "Let's have a look at the body now."

Unlike the rest of the house, Margaret Brownfield's bedroom was chockfull of photos and other mementoes. Her walls were covered with pictures of Amanda from birth to present. She'd created the same visual timeline for Maddie. There were no photos of men. If the grandmother had had a husband, she hadn't kept a single photo of him. At least there was none on display.

Margaret Brownfield had been a small woman. She had died in her bed. Her mint green flannel nightgown showed no signs of blood. The covers were drawn around her as if she'd gone to sleep and just never woke up. Her long gray hair was draped across the pillow. She would have looked completely peaceful if not for the fact that her eyes were wide open. The petechial hemorrhaging in the eyes and on the face suggested asphyxiation. The extra pillow, lying next to the one where the victim's head rested, was likely what the killer used since there were no ligature marks on the throat. There were no other visible signs of trauma. On the left side of the victim's forehead was an imprint as if someone had kissed her there—someone wearing deep red lipstick.

"You think Amanda killed her mom, and then dropped off her daughter because she was about to do something we haven't heard about yet?"

"Possibly." Jess pointed to the lipstick imprint. The woman in the surveillance video with Maddie had worn deep red lip color. "At the very least, she kissed her goodbye." She looked around the room again. "We need the make and license plate information on the vehicle she's driving. We also need a photo of the boyfriend and what he drives, along with a list of friends for both. Whatever Amanda Brownfield is up to, we need to find her."

Whether Amanda killed her mother or not, she no doubt knew who did.

Lori quickly compiled Jess's requests into her electronic notepad. Jess would take her pencil and pad any day over putting everything into a place where it could just disappear if you hit the wrong key. She'd had that happen before.

"Let's see if there's a basement or cellar." Jess hadn't discovered an access inside the house but there could be one outside. She headed for the kitchen. A lot of old houses had basements or cellars. Either one made a good place for hiding things... or other bodies. At least one member of this family definitely had things to hide.

The screen door on the rear of house groaned when it opened and then closed with a thwack. There was no back porch, just a few steps that led down to the yard. Jess sat down on the top step and removed her shoes covers. Lori did the same. A large vegetable garden had wilted in the heat.

Jess walked around the house looking for a basement access but found nothing. Maybe there wasn't a basement after all. There was definitely a crawlspace. No one was going to like her when she requested a search of that area.

"Chief."

Jess turned to Lori who was checking her cell. "Harper says we need to come down to the barn."

The barn was next on Jess's agenda. "Maybe they found the boyfriend."

The walk to the barn was a bit less treacherous than the one along the driveway. Jess only had a shoe heel sink into the soft dirt once. With fewer of those huge trees in the back, the sun had a chance to remind her that her antiperspirant was failing miserably. Two deputies waited outside the barn. Hayes met them at the open door.

"We have another body?" If the boyfriend was still alive, he could be working with Amanda. If he was dead, he wasn't going to be any help to the investigation.

Hayes shook his head. "Don't know if this means anything, but you need to see for yourself."

Inside the barn, a few bales of hay sat abandoned near the gardening and yard implements. There was no tractor or plows or anything mechanized. The barn wasn't that large. Off to the left, where Harper and Foster waited, there was a second door, this one as wide and tall as the first. A gray tarp covered something large parked just inside that door.

Jess spotted a tire peeking from under the tarp. A vehicle of some sort. "Do you recognize the vehicle?" she asked the sheriff.

He shrugged. "I'm running the license plate through the system. It expired a hell of a long time ago so I can't guarantee any results."

Harper and the lieutenant removed the tarp, revealing an old blue car.

"Cadillac," Foster said. "I'm guessing thirty-five or so years old. License plate expired thirty-two years ago. Looks in mint condition except for this one thing."

As if Mother Nature wanted to warn Jess that something evil was coming, thunder boomed and the light tap, tap, tap of rain sounded on the metal roof. She couldn't remember the last time she'd watched a weather forecast. Obviously, she should have this morning but she'd had other things on her mind.

Jess moved toward where Harper and the others waited, and then she froze. Someone had taken a can of spray paint to the side of the Cadillac. Jess's heart stumbled, seemed to stop beating at all as she read the words.

*It should have been you, Jessie Lee.*

# CHAPTER ELEVEN

Jess piled her wet hair up and fastened it with a clip.
She stared at her reflection in the mirror and shook
her head. She had ruined her favorite Mary Janes.
By five o'clock, the rain had started to come down
in sheets. Her red suit was soaking wet and splat-
tered with mud but her shoes were beyond repair.
Jess shuffled out of the bathroom and went to the
window that looked out over the driveway. Still no
Dan. He'd called to say he had a late meeting. The
BPD cruiser assigned to watch over her sat right
next to the Audi she was no longer allowed to drive.
There would be another cruiser on the street but
she couldn't see it from here.

Rubbing her eyes with her fists, she tried to
block the images from that damned wall at the farmhouse. Whoever Amanda Brownfield was, she was
connected to Spears. No question. Gant was coming
tomorrow. He wanted to have a look personally. She
doubted it would do any good. Unless the forensic

team found something Jess and her team hadn't, it was a waste of time and money.

All she had was speculation. There was the lipstick imprint, but that alone didn't prove anything other than the fact that Amanda had likely seen her mother just before or after her murder. Maybe she kissed the woman goodbye and left before the killer showed up. Or maybe she discovered the body and freaked out. Amanda Brownfield could be a serial killer groupie for all Jess knew. The articles she'd cut from newspapers and printed from the Internet might have nothing to do with Jess. The woman may have been obsessed with the Player long before she saw the name Jess Harris in print. The photos she'd discovered on the Internet may have been tracked down after the big media explosion in July. There was no way to be certain since any dates that might have printed with the material had been trimmed away before the articles were posted on the woman's bedroom wall.

None of which explained how she'd gotten her hands on that photo of Jess and Wesley. Since neither of them had a Facebook or a Twitter account, they didn't go around posting selfies.

What Jess needed was to find Amanda Brownfield or maybe her boyfriend, Brock Clements. There was a BOLO out for both. Jess and her team had just started interviewing neighbors when the deluge kicked into full force. The houses along that road were spaced acres apart. Not surprisingly, no one appeared to know anything other than what they saw passing on the road, which was how they'd known Clements was involved with Amanda.

Sheriff Foster had promised to have the list of friends and acquaintances of both suspects to Jess by tomorrow afternoon. He had given her carte blanche in his county. Frankly, he'd made his feelings on the issue abundantly clear. He was more than happy for her to have this case. Who could blame him?

The news had been relayed to Wettermark at Child Services. Maddie Brownfield needed to be in protective custody. With her grandmother murdered and her mother unaccounted for, the child could be in danger. Although Jess hated to see Maddie moved from the Graham home, the situation was too unpredictable to put that family and all those other children in danger. If Amanda Brownfield suddenly decided she wanted her child back, there was no telling what she might do. Jess didn't have enough information about her to assess what she might be capable of.

Wettermark had waited until after dark to move Maddie. Jess wrestled with whether or not to stop in and check on the little girl, but she wasn't sure doing so was a good idea. No matter how careful she was or the evasive maneuvers taken, she couldn't be sure those Spears had tailing her wouldn't end up finding the location. It wasn't worth the risk.

Per doctor's orders, she was supposed to be putting work aside once she was home for the night but that wasn't happening tonight. Not after what she'd seen in Jackson County today. She moved to the makeshift case board she'd created on the wall—her homework board. Like the one at the office, Maddie's photo was there as well as the timeline from the moment she had been dropped off on Sixth Avenue until the present. A photo of her mother and grandmother, as well as a DMV shot of the boyfriend, had been added. Lori had taken numerous photos of the wall in Amanda Brownfield's bedroom. Jess had printed those and posted them beneath Amanda's photo. A photo of the car, now at Jefferson County's forensic lab, had been posted as well. Jess wondered if the Cadillac had belonged to Margaret's husband. The license plate had last been registered to Lawrence Howard. So far, that was the only record of Lawrence they'd found. He was listed as the father on Amanda's birth record, but there was no marriage license between him and Margaret recorded in Jackson County. Margaret had still used her maiden name. Maybe the two were never married.

If Lawrence was Amanda's father, why hadn't there been any photos? Maybe he'd abandoned the family, leaving the kind of bitterness that made Margaret destroy all reminders. He could be buried on the farm somewhere. Stranger things happened. Margaret may have discovered he was cheating on her or molesting their daughter—which might explain, to some degree, Amanda's life style and penchant for criminal activities.

How had Amanda become involved with Spears? It seemed so farfetched. They'd found no indication she'd ever lived in the Richmond, Virginia, area. SpearNet, Spears's corporation, was headquartered in Richmond. Then again, Spears had a wide and varied following. Amanda may have run into him on the Internet. There were no computers in the home so she would have had to go to a library or a friend's. Or she could very well be nothing more than a wannabe following the Spears storyline. The media had gone to great lengths to keep the world informed about Spears and his twisted following as well as the Birmingham cop who, unfortunately, was the focus of his current demented scheme.

"Yay me." Jess hugged her arms around her waist and headed to the fridge. She was starving. She couldn't wait for Dan any longer.

Her cell clanged and Jess rushed back to sofa where she'd left it. Hopefully, Dan was calling to say he was headed home with something scrumptious for dinner. Not Dan. Jess frowned. The caller ID showed the number for the cop outside watching her apartment.

"Harris." She wandered back to the window. Another vehicle was in the driveway but she couldn't determine the make.

"Chief, there's two ladies out here who say you're expecting them. I've checked their ID's. Sylvia Baron and—"

"Doctor Sylvia Baron," a voice in the background corrected.

"Dr. Sylvia Baron," the officer amended, "and that reporter Gina Coleman."

*Great.* "Send them up." Jess sighed. She wasn't dressed for company and she was starving, but she couldn't turn them away. Not if she wanted Sylvia to agree to drive over to Jackson County and have a look at Margaret Brownfield's body. The Jackson County coroner bucked at releasing the body to Jefferson County, but he did agree to allow a look from an outsider. Not that he could have stopped the request but it was better to play nice than to get into a legal battle. *You catch more flies with honey than you do with vinegar.*

Jess hadn't been gone from the south so long that she'd forgotten everything she had learned growing up here.

She tossed her phone aside and tugged at her t-shirt. She looked a mess. Her lounge pants were practically old enough to be considered vintage and the tee was her favorite, which meant both were well on their way to being worn out. Wouldn't be the first time Sylvia or Gina had seen her in a completely natural state. No makeup, hair undone and looking thrift store chic. For that matter, every piece of furniture she owned except that comfy mattress had come from a thrift store.

After disarming the security system and unlocking the deadbolts, she opened the door to a beaming Sylvia Baron who, as usual, looked exactly like a cover model half her age. Those new red highlights she was sporting didn't hurt either. Jess had meant to ask her about the subtle change in hair color last week, but she and Sylvia hadn't been on the best of terms. Still, if Jess didn't like her so much she would hate her for looking so good all the time.

Sylvia held up a pizza box and a bottle of wine. "Dan said he was going to be late tonight. We thought we'd bring you dinner."

Gina Coleman, dressed in workout clothes, elbowed her way around Sylvia and pushed right past Jess. "Drop the ruse, Sylvia. Tell her why we're really here."

Jess looked from one to the other. "Tell me later, I'm starving."

Sylvia marched to the table with the food. Jess locked up and tried to come up with an explanation to give these two for why she wouldn't be partaking of the wine—no matter how tempting. Before she could summon a clever excuse, her attention settled on Gina. She sat on the sofa, slumped over her smart phone. This was totally out of character for Birmingham's award winning celebrity journalist—and one of Dan's ex-lovers. Jess hadn't seen her looking this depressed since she found out her younger sister was involved with murder.

"Okay, I change my mind. What's going on?" As hungry as Jess was, something was up with these two and, for once, she suspected it wasn't trouble related to her.

"Dinner is served," Sylvia announced, ignoring Jess. "Where's your corkscrew, Harris?"

Jess walked over to the kitchen side of her apartment. Like her office, it was just one big room. She opened a drawer. "Really," she said, "what's happened?" Gina Coleman was intelligent, hard-working, gorgeous, and had a nose for a story. Tonight, for some reason, she looked very much the way Jess did when she woke up in the morning—like hell.

Sylvia grabbed the corkscrew and went to work on opening the wine. Jess gathered a couple of bottles of water from the fridge and offered one to Gina. The last Jess had heard, Gina had decided to back off her alcohol consumption. Gina accepted the bottle without looking up or even saying thanks.

Since no one wanted to talk, Jess went for a slice of pizza. It smelled wonderful and was loaded with everything but the kitchen sink, the way she liked it. She sank into a chair at the table as she tore into the slice of hot, spicy perfection.

Sylvia didn't sit until she'd tossed back a glass of wine then she promptly declared, "Gina is gay. That asshole Stevens just outed her on Facebook."

The sound of Gina's phone hitting the wall made Jess jump. The reporter stamped over to the table, grabbed a slice of pizza and started devouring it.

"Wow." Jess wasn't sure it was safe to say anything else. And she'd thought she had a big secret. This was the Bible Belt, folks were still behind the curve on tolerance and acceptance when it came to alternative lifestyles.

"Precisely," Sylvia acknowledged, and then she frowned. "Haven't you seen the news tonight? It's on every damned channel."

"I try not to watch." Jess shook her head and focused on her pizza. The truth was she didn't care to see or hear anything the reporters had to say about her. She was okay with the expose Gina had done, there was a mutual goal behind that move. The rest Jess had no desire to filter.

"Stevens set the whole thing up," Sylvia stated with complete certainty. "Someone comes on his Facebook page and asks why he hasn't done anything as a TV reporter on being gay in Birmingham. He raved on for a bit before suggesting Stevens was intolerant or else he'd report on the city's other minority. In his reply, Stevens goes on endlessly about how he believes everyone has the right to live their lives their own way. In fact, he said, one of his dearest friends and most admired colleagues is gay. Then he posted a picture of Gina."

Jess couldn't deny being a little startled. Not that she minded. To each their own. She turned to Gina. "I'm sorry he told the world before you were ready."

Gina shrugged and reached for a second slice. Jess would bet her beloved Coach Bleecker bag that Gina Coleman hadn't eaten a second portion of anything since she was twelve years old.

"The station is weighing whether they can afford to keep me," she said, disgusted. "The backlash could drastically affect ratings. They wouldn't say it, but I know how they think."

Sylvia shook her head. "You give everything you have to give and then at the first sign of controversy suddenly nothing matters."

The medical examiner had lost her husband when he had an affair with a younger woman willing to have children. Despite the tragic ending to that love triangle, Sylvia was clearly still bitter and determined to have a younger paramour of her own. Jess's only problem with the doctor's decision was that the younger paramour was a member of her team.

Proof positive that Jess wasn't the only one with such a screwed up personal life.

"From the day I returned to Birmingham," she said, deciding to throw in her two cents worth, "every aspect of my life has been in the news." She laughed dryly. "I figure it can't get any worse than it already has and I lived through it. You will too."

Gina grabbed a napkin and dabbed her lips. "My career in Birmingham is over."

Jess had been there too, but she opted not to remind Gina. Instead, for the next ten minutes Jess and Sylvia attempted to assure Gina that this was the twenty-first century and being gay was completely acceptable and respected.

"Besides," Sylvia tacked on, "you can't be fired for being gay. Your boss certainly can't cite your ratings. You are the most watched reporter in Birmingham. This city loves you whether you like dick or not."

Jess almost choked on her water. She bit her lip to prevent saying she was pretty sure Gina enjoyed it occasionally. After all, she and Dan had an ongoing friends-with-benefits relationship until Jess returned. She couldn't help wondering if Dan had heard the news.

"You're right." Gina hugged her knees to her chest. "They can't fire me, but they can start grooming someone else for the spotlight." She shook her head. "Hard work and luck only gets you so far in this business. A station has to be behind you. The powers that be have to want to make you a star and to keep you there."

That, unfortunately, was true of any profession. A certain amount of politics was the bane of all careers. Jess doubted that would ever change.

Sylvia poured herself another glass of wine. "Why aren't you having any, Harris?" Sylvia jerked her head toward Gina. "I'm trying to respect Gina's need to avoid a path toward alcoholism—even if she has the perfect excuse to fall off the wagon. What's your excuse?"

To her utter consternation, Jess's brain opted to go on hiatus at that moment. "I…" Jess shrugged. "I need to keep my head clear for this case."

Sylvia scoffed. "You've had wine before when you were working on a case. Are you two trying to make me look bad?" She made a face that warned she would not tolerate any such attempts. "Don't even start. If you hacked up bodies for a living, you would drink too."

Valid point. Jess looked from one to the other. These two women were her friends. She could tell them about the pregnancy and ask that they keep it quiet. She was certain they would honor her request. Nah, she couldn't risk it. Besides, she had to tell her team first—and Dan's parents. Oh God, she so dreaded his mother finding out.

A change of subject to something safer was in order. "Do you think Stevens did this because of the Spears story? Since he's not a better reporter than you, he's clearly desperate, and maybe this was his stab at getting a minute in the spotlight." The more Jess thought about it, the angrier she got. "If he was half as good as you, he wouldn't have to resort to such underhanded tactics."

"Hear, hear," Sylvia lifted her glass. "I couldn't have said it better myself."

"I think," Jess was on a roll now, "what you need to shut down this little frenzy is the inside track on what's happening with my latest murder investigation. We believe Spears is involved in this one too." The words were out before Jess could consider what she was offering. She felt a little guilty that maybe using Gina to help with her situation from time to time might be what placed her into the line of fire with Stevens. Envy was a nasty business.

Besides, what were friends for?

Gina got up and walked to the homework board Jess had made. "You might be right. This could be what I need to stay on top." She set her hands on her hips. "I could ride along with you and the team. Get into the trenches and away from all this other unpleasantness."

Jess wanted to kick herself. "Ride alongs can be risky."

Inspiration dawned in the reporter's expression. "Seriously, this could be great." She rushed back to the table and sat down next to Jess. "You could save my career."

"Of course she'll include you," Sylvia said. "That's what friends do."

Jess mustered up a smile. "Absolutely." She gave a nod of finality more to solidify the decision for herself than for anyone else. "I'm heading to Scottsboro at six sharp in the morning. It's a two hour drive. You're welcome to follow." The logistics would be a huge pain and no one on her team was going to be happy. No cop liked having a member of the media looking over her shoulder.

What had she done? Jess kicked the doubts aside. She had supported a friend who was going to help her prove Dan was being framed in Allen's disappearance.

"That's settled." Sylvia gingerly picked up a slice of pizza. "So, aren't you at all curious if it's true?"

Sylvia directed the question at Jess. Jess frowned as if she didn't understand. "If what's true?"

Sylvia laughed. "The story about Gina."

Gina rolled her eyes. "You're such a bitch, Sylvia."

Jess shrugged. "It's irrelevant to me." She decided to give Sylvia something else to ruminate on. "The same as you picking a young man scarcely more than half your age. You like your partners young, she likes hers female. Who has the right to judge?"

Sylvia narrowed her eyes. "I thought you were against my relationship with Chad."

Chad not Cook. Jess struggled to cap her rising irritation. "Only because he's a member of my team. I don't want any work issues cropping up."

Sylvia's lips stretched into a wicked grin. "The only thing that's up when he and I are together is—"

"No one wants to hear that!" Gina held up her hands and waved them back and forth. "Subject change, please."

As annoyed as Jess was with Sylvia pursuing the relationship with Cook, at least she'd accomplished her goal and was more than happy to move on. "How's Nina?" Jess had no idea where that question had come from, but there it was.

Sylvia blinked, apparently as startled as Jess by the unexpected inquiry. "There's been no change in her condition. We're moving her to a new hospital in two weeks. We're hopeful about the treatment there." She took a sip of her wine but the move came too late to prevent Jess seeing her lips tremble. "Thank you for asking."

Nina Baron, Sylvia's sister, had once been Dan's wife. Ten years ago when Jess had run into Dan at the Hoover Publix on Christmas Eve, he'd just gone through the divorce from Nina. Nina had been in a private care facility since. Dan hadn't known about Nina's mental illness until she'd tried to kill him with his own handgun. The family had kept that dark secret extremely well. Nina had barely spoken since that horrifying event. She'd retreated inside herself and no one seemed able to reach her.

Silence lapsed while they finished off the pizza. When Jess had been a teenager in Birmingham, her only friend had been Buddy Corlew. She and Lil had been muddling through foster care. Unlike Sylvia and Gina, they'd hardly gotten more than a glance at what life was like for girls whose families were rich and sent them to the best private school in the state. The same one Dan had attended.

Now, they were friends. Life certainly took some strange turns.

Even stranger was that it required all three of them, each bringing her own expertise, to keep this city a safer place. Funny how things worked out that way.

Jess had spent most of her life being a loner with maybe one person she actually called a friend. At that moment, she realized she wanted more for her child. She wanted her child to be surrounded by family and friends right from the beginning.

Maybe Dan was right. They should get married and invite the world to celebrate the occasion.

Okay, it was official. The lack of wine was taking a toll. Or maybe it was hormones. Her body was in gestation mode and everything else was going to pot. The next thing she knew she'd be going to afternoon tea and joining the local Women's Club and the PTA. Jess redirected her errant thoughts. Clearly, she was edging toward hysteria.

Not true. She wanted her child to have a far better childhood than hers and Lil's. Nothing wrong with that goal.

As much as she wanted to ensure that end, the bottom line was, if she didn't find a way to stop Spears she wouldn't have a life.

# CHAPTER TWELVE

"It's a good thing you warned me to dress for nosing around on a farm." Gina Coleman wiped the side of her running shoes on a clump of grass, but the mud wasn't coming off to her satisfaction.

Yesterday's downpour had turned into today's mud pit. Since this morning's agenda was about searching the property for whatever they could find, in addition to interviewing neighbors, fitting attire was essential.

Not to mention Jess was still annoyed that her favorite pair of shoes had lost the battle with the elements yesterday. She wasn't sacrificing any more of her already meager wardrobe. After her motel room, along with every article of clothing she'd brought to Birmingham, had been destroyed a few weeks ago, she hadn't found the time to pull together a decent wardrobe. On the other hand, her limited shopping since the vandalism was probably for the best considering she would need an entirely different wardrobe for the coming months. Maybe jeans and sneakers would become SPU's new dress code. The BPD logos on the t-shirts were official enough.

Everyone but Hayes had been happy to get the heads up about today's suggested casual attire. Somehow, the man managed to make jeans and a polo look elegant. Even his Sketchers were leather. Maybe he was still more lawyer wannabe than he realized. Suited Jess just fine. It didn't hurt to have a detective with a law degree under his belt, particularly now. As long as he learned to fit in, preferably sooner than later.

"Contrary to popular belief," Jess informed the reporter, "this job isn't always glamorous."

"I guess we have that in common." Gina motioned for her cameraman to come closer. "Did you get a good pan of the house and yard?"

Before he could answer, Jess warned, "Remember, Officer Cook goes where you go and don't touch anything. Keep the gloves on and, if you go inside, wear the shoe covers."

"I won't touch anything," Gina promised. "I won't air anything without your prior approval."

Jess couldn't decide if the invitation for Gina to come along had been a stroke of brilliance or a lapse in sanity. Either way, they were here and she had work to do. "Detective Wells, let's start where we left off with the interviews."

Lori scanned the yard. "I'll let Hayes know we're ready to go."

There was that insecurity again. "We don't need the lieutenant. He and Harper should carry on with their search of the grounds. You and I can handle the interviews."

Visibly reluctant, Lori headed for her Mustang. Jess climbed into the passenger seat and watched the reporter get started. Gina stood beneath one of the big Oak trees and spoke to the camera. Shooting an opening, Jess supposed. This was definitely a first for her. She'd never worked with a reporter at the scene. They were typically outside the perimeter, like those held back by the sheriff's roadblocks a half a mile down the road in either direction.

The department would likely catch some flak for showing preference. Jess would deal with that when the time came.

"Sheriff Foster sent Harper a list of people who've recently been involved with Amanda and her boyfriend in one way or another. He said neither of our suspects has any real friends to speak of." Lori passed her cell phone to Jess. "Harper forwarded the list to me, if you want to take a look."

As Lori backed out of the long, rutted drive, Jess scanned the names and comments Foster had made about each. She hesitated on one name. Slade Evans. Former boyfriend. Two arrests for assault, one misdemeanor drug possession.

"Let's pay this Slade Evans a visit," Jess suggested. The closest two neighbors had already insisted they hadn't heard or seen anything. They had no connections socially or otherwise to the Brownfield family. Jess doubted they'd get anymore than that out of the neighbors who lived even farther from the farm.

The local radio and television stations had been running photos of the two suspects and asking the community for help. No useful tips so far.

"What's the address for Evans?"

"Harbin's Auto Repair on Main Street. Evans is a mechanic there."

Lori stalled before backing out onto the road, but she didn't look at Jess. "We should have Hayes or Harper come along if we're going into town."

"We'll have a BPD cop right behind us. I need the rest of the team at the scene."

Lori nodded, still avoiding Jess's gaze as she backed out onto the road. Jess mulled over the things she could say but she'd said them all before. Undoubtedly, Lori would come to terms with what happened in her own time. Another wave of guilt washed over Jess as she pondered the secret she was keeping from her friend. Of all the people she had come to know since her return to Birmingham, Lori was the one Jess considered a close friend. She didn't want anything to ruin that.

Trusting Lori wasn't an issue. Jess opened her mouth to tell her, but Lori spoke first. "Chet scheduled his surgery for the week after next." She glanced at Jess as she navigated the car past the roadblock. Reporters waved and shouted questions but Jess ignored them. She had nothing to give anyone.

"He'll be out of work for a few days, maybe a week. If that's a problem, he can reschedule."

Jess was glad to hear Harper was getting the vasectomy reversal taken care of. That secret could have torn him and Lori apart. Although, Lori didn't sound as excited about the news as Jess would have expected. "I'm glad that issue worked out. I'm sure we can manage without him for a few days." Admittedly, it wouldn't be easy. Jess relied heavily on each of her detectives, as well as Cook. She had to remember to see that Harper started prepping Cook for the detective's exam as soon as things calmed down. He deserved the promotion at the earliest possible date.

"I guess I'm glad too."

Jess frowned. Somehow, the detective didn't sound glad. "You sure about that?"

Lori squeezed the steering wheel more tightly. "The reversal comes with a condition. Once the surgery is done, scar tissue can develop and create problems, so they recommend no waiting to start a family. I'm not sure I'm ready for kids." She shook her head. "We're not even married. We're just getting this relationship off the ground and his ex-wife is acting like a crazy bitch." She paused to draw in a shuddering breath. "Even if what she did was best for Chester. It's just a mess."

This was the moment. Lori needed to feel as if someone else understood. Someone career oriented like her. Someone like Jess. Someone in a similar position.

"You think you have problems," Jess said, going for offhanded but failing miserably. "I just found out I'm pregnant."

Lori stared at her. "What?"

Jess cleared her throat and pointed to the road.

Lori jerked her attention forward. "You're pregnant?" Her voice rose an octave or two as she spoke.

"Three or four pregnancy tests and one doctor say so," Jess rolled her eyes, "but I'm still holding out hope it's a false alarm."

Lori maneuvered the Mustang into the first parking lot she came to, shoved the gearshift into park, and turned to Jess. "Are you okay?"

Jess shrugged. "Physically, I think so. They're checking me for Wilson's disease, but otherwise I'm in great health." Except for being old. No need to mention that part. Too depressing.

"You know what I mean," Lori said pointedly.

The BPD cruiser eased up next to them. Jess waved at the cop behind the wheel to let him know they were fine. "It was a shock." She turned back to Lori. "Evidently around the time frame that you were missing I did a little missing myself. I skipped a couple or three pills and here I am. Pregnant."

"Oh my God." Lori pressed a hand to her chest. "What about the chief? How's he handling this?"

"He wants to get married today and tell his folks." She smiled, worked hard at restraining the emotion that immediately burned her eyes. "He's thrilled."

Excitement crept into her friend's face. "Does anyone else know? Can I tell Chet?"

"Only my sister. I told her yesterday after I saw the doctor." Jess relaxed a little. It felt good to have that secret off her chest. "I don't mind if Harper knows as long as he doesn't start hovering more. If you can believe it, Dan's working hard to give me a little more space. I think he might be afraid I'll have a meltdown or something." Jess frowned. "Oh, and Hayes knows. He figured out I'd bought a pregnancy test."

"Yeah, he's nosy like that," Lori gripped.

What was this thing between Hayes and everyone else on the team? Wasn't he friends with Lori? Not the time to ask, Jess decided. One startling revelation at a time was more than enough.

Lori turned her hands up. "This is… exciting news." She smiled then. The first real one Jess had seen from her in days. "Honestly, I'm torn between being ecstatic and completely stunned."

"Welcome to my world," Jess admitted. "My hormones are working against me. Spears is threatening everyone I care about." She sagged under the weight of it all. "I'm terrified."

"I didn't think about all that." Lori reached across the console and squeezed Jess's hand. "Here I am worrying about whether I want to commit to have Chet's child in the near future and you're dealing with Spears and you're already having a baby. Is there anything I can do?"

"There is." Jess looked her in the eyes. "You can go back to being the cop you were before Friday."

Lori's expression fell. "Oh." She looked away. "I'm working on it, but the truth is I don't know if I can trust myself again. You could've been killed." Her attention dropped to Jess's waist before rising to meet her eyes once more. "Your child could have died, because of *my* mistake."

"Eventually, you'll see that you didn't do anything wrong," Jess countered. "The sooner the better for all concerned." She faced forward. Arguing the point wouldn't change Lori's mind. She had to find her own way back. "Let's get this interview done."

HARBIN'S AUTO REPAIR, 10:10 AM

Darren Harbin, the owner of the shop, agreed to lend Jess the employee break room for questioning Slade Evans.

Evans was forty, tall, and broad shouldered. Evidently, he enjoyed showing off how much time he spent working out since he wore one of those tank top style t-shirts that exposed his bulging, tattooed biceps. He sported a buzz cut and an indifferent attitude. At least he was willing to talk.

"Your relationship with Amanda ended in February, is that correct?" Jess studied her notes. "After Valentine's Day." That hadn't been a very good holiday for Jess this year either. She'd been reassigned the Spears case and had foolishly thought that was a positive thing.

"That's right. I would've ended it sooner but she owed me fifty bucks. She wasn't gonna have the money until she got her tax refund. She picks up a job here and there just to make sure she gets that earned income whatever for the kid."

"Who was her last employer?"

"Restaurant out on 35. She worked there for a couple months until she got in a big brawl with the night manager. Beat the hell out of the woman." Evans leaned forward and braced his forearms on the table. "Amanda's crazy, in case you ain't figured that out already. I mean, total, bat shit crazy. She can be all sweet and lovey-dovey one minute and ready to cut your throat the next."

"Is that your opinion or are you speaking from experience," Jess prodded.

"Experience," he assured her, "definitely. I woke up one night and she was sitting in the bed staring at me. Might've been all right if she hadn't been holding a butcher knife." He shook his head and made a face. "Besides, all she talks about is serial killers and murders. She loves that shit."

"Have you ever known her to do more than rough someone up?" Jess placed her badge on the table just to remind him who he was talking to. "The statement you're giving is the same as if you were in a courtroom testifying. Think carefully before you continue." That wasn't exactly true but he wouldn't know the difference.

"I can't prove it but a couple times when she was wasted she bragged about killing people. I thought it was just her trying to be a bad ass. She likes attention. If she doesn't get it, she gets pissed. I wouldn't want her pissed at me." He leaned back, showed his hands. "I knew I was done with her when she started talking about having sex with a serial killer.

That *player* guy. He's all she talks about. She acts like she knows him or something. I'm telling you she's nuts."

Tension squeezed a little tighter around Jess's chest. "Did she tell you she'd spoken to him or met him?"

He shrugged. "Nah. At first, I thought he was more of her crazy talk. I'd never heard of him. I figured she made him up. She does that too. She has this big complicated story about her old man." He smirked. "My momma said her daddy abandoned her. You try telling Amanda that and she'll scratch your eyes out."

"When did you realize Amanda wasn't talking about a fictitious serial killer this time?"

"When I saw all that shit on the news, I asked her about it. She said she could have told me all that before it happened."

Jess readied her pencil, hoped the man didn't see her hand shake. "I'll need your mother's name and contact information."

"She don't know nothing about Amanda except that she's crazy. Hell, she killed her own mamma, didn't she?"

"But your mother can vouch for what you've told me, isn't that right?" Jess asked. "You said you were home with your mother last night? If I can't confirm your statement, then you have no alibi."

He rattled off Connie Evans's telephone number and address.

"Mr. Evans, is there anything at all you can tell us about Amanda's current boyfriend, Brock Clements?"

"He used to work over at Vulcan driving a truck. Friend of mine works there too. He said Brock hasn't been to work in a while. You could check at the Oasis. Amanda likes to hang out there. She was there Saturday night celebrating the Tide's win over Arkansas." He grunted. "I don't know why she thought that game was something to celebrate. Anybody can beat Arkansas. It's Florida they better worry about."

"I appreciate your cooperation, Mr. Evans." Jess stood and passed him her card. "If you think of anything else, please call me."

"You know that lipstick she wears?"

Jess collected her bag. "I know it's red. Why?"

"It's Killer Red," he said with a grin. "She told me it made her feel good to wear it because she's a killer." He shrugged. "I guess I should've believed her."

"Perhaps so," Jess agreed. "You said you saw her on Saturday at a place called the Oasis, I'll need that address."

"Highway 79, going out of town toward Guntersville. You might catch the manager there. His name's Doug Sanders. He'll tell you she's crazy, too."

Jess was nearly convinced he was right about that part. "Did Amanda ever mention seeing a psychiatrist or seeking any other mental health support?"

He lifted his chin and made one of those aha faces as if he'd just recalled something important. "Now that you mention it, she's talked about a shrink before. I can't remember his name. One of those quacks over at the mental health center. She used to laugh about how she freaked him out with her stories." Evans looked straight at Jess then. "Does she freak you out? You know she bleached her hair so she could look like you."

Jess stilled. "How do you know she wanted to look like me?"

He grinned. "I guess I forgot to tell you. You're the only other thing she ever talked about besides Spears and murders. I thought she made you up too until I saw your pretty face splashed across the news."

"You didn't think to mention that until now?"

He shrugged. "I didn't want to say anything until I knew."

Jess's patience was at an end. "Knew what, Mr. Evans?"

"Whether you were anything like her." He eyed Jess for several seconds too long. "But I guess you're not."

"Why would you think I was like her?"

"She said something about y'all being alike, that's all."

"Thank you, Mr. Evans. We may need to call on you again."

He glanced from Jess to Lori and back. "Anytime."

Once they were in the Mustang en route to the Oasis, Jess did a search for the city's mental health center. "While I'm questioning the club manager, assuming we can catch him," she said to Lori, "try getting me an appointment with the doctor Amanda was seeing at the mental health center. I'd really like to talk to him today."

"You think he'll talk to you?"

"Probably not but it never hurts to ask." Jess could learn a number of things from his reaction to her questions. If there were reason to worry that Amanda was capable of murder, she would see it in the doctor's eyes.

OASIS. 11:30 A.M.

"Yeah, she was here." Doug Sanders said as he loaded the cooler behind the bar with bottles of beer. "She and that Brock guy she's got wrapped around her little finger were here until just before closing."

"Have you seen either of them since?" Jess asked.

Lori joined them at the bar and gave Jess a nod. If the doctor Amanda had been seeing had agreed to see Jess maybe he would cooperate to the extent possible. That was always a plus. Doctor-Patient privilege wasn't easy to get around but anything he could offer could prove useful.

"Nope," Sanders said, "and I'm pissed too. Brock was supposed to help me with some plumbing issues yesterday and he didn't show. He's not answering his cell and nobody's seen him since Saturday. You can't count on nobody these days."

"Does he make it a habit of disappearing like this?"

"Not that I know of. Why don't you ask his mother? She lives over in the projects close to the hospital. Brock's one of them guys with that "failure to launch syndrome." He still lives with her. She might know where he is."

Jess wanted to interview the boyfriend's mother anyway since she was the one to find Margaret Brownfield's body. Maybe she had some idea where her son would hide if he were in trouble.

If he was still breathing.

# CHAPTER THIRTEEN

Dan had waited for half an hour. Pratt evidently derived great pleasure from wasting his time. Dan had rushed to the mayor's office on numerous other occasions for an emergency meeting only to end up sitting here twiddling his thumbs.

Pratt's secretary grimaced. "I'm so sorry you're having to wait, Chief. No sooner than he requested this meeting, he was called away. He hoped to be back before you arrived, apparently that didn't work out."

Dan resurrected a decent smile for the woman. This wasn't her fault. Pratt was yanking his chain. He had been against Jess coming onboard with the department from the beginning and things had only gone downhill from there. Since Dan refused to cooperate with his desires, Pratt was no longer happy with Dan either.

It was no surprise the man had jumped on the bandwagon against Dan in the Allen investigation.

When the mayor didn't get his way, he sought opportunities to remove the problem. Dan had become a problem.

He hadn't heard from Jess since about ten this morning. He hoped she was being careful. He didn't want her out in the field but she was determined to do the job—the job he'd talked her into taking. He supposed he couldn't have his cake and eat it too. Be that as it may, things were different now. She was carrying his child. *Their child.* He needed her to be more careful than ever.

He'd rushed home after a long, drawn out meeting with the city planners last night and found her asleep on the sofa. Thankfully, Sylvia and Gina had kept her company for most of the evening. It was good to have friends he could count on. He rubbed his jaw. Last night's big news was all about Gina's secret sexual preference. He'd been surprised at first, but hey, she had a right to be who she was. No one should have to pretend to be someone he or she wasn't. He was glad Jess had found a way to include her in the Jackson County investigation. Getting Gina out of the city for the day would give her a break from those hounding her for confirmation.

Dan checked the time again. Where in the hell was Pratt?

Just when Dan was ready to walk, Pratt breezed into his private lobby. "Sorry to keep you waiting, Chief." He slowed long enough to gesture to his door. "Come in, please." To his secretary he said, "Hold my calls."

Dan took his usual seat in front of Pratt's desk and waited for him to settle into his. For more than a decade, he had served as the liaison between this office and the one he now held. He'd had the utmost respect for Joseph Pratt in the beginning. The mayor, among others, had hoped to groom Dan for moving up in the local political world. Pratt had his eye on the governorship. He'd hoped Dan would be elected as mayor and perhaps eventually into higher office.

*Time changes all things.* Dan had come to realize that politics was not for him. The level he tolerated as chief of police was more than enough. He no longer had any respect for or cared to waste his time or energy dealing with those who assumed justice should take a backseat to their perception of the greater good. Over the years, he and Pratt had come to a new understanding: they had little, if anything, in common. Sharing the same social circles was the extent of their common interests and even that ground was shaky.

If turning a blind eye on occasion and choosing power and wealth were more important than justice, Dan wanted no part of higher office. He was happy where he was. Trouble was his position as chief of police often conflicted with what the mayor and his allies wanted.

Tough. Dan wasn't budging anymore.

"I've been in a meeting with the city comptroller this morning," Pratt announced. He studied the documents on his desk for a moment before leaning back in his chair to scrutinize Dan. "The budget over-runs for your department this quarter are staggering. Round the clock surveillance on no less than a dozen people." He turned his hands up in question. "Where do you expect these additional funds are going to come from? Are you prepared to cut back on person-nel? Training? You aren't thinking, man!"

There was an issue Dan hadn't expected today. "I'm well aware of the department's budget over-runs at the moment. But we've been careful the past three or four years. We're in good shape. I'm on top of this." Dan had met with the comptroller last week. "I was assured the budget's on target."

Pratt scoffed. "I hardly think so. The depart-ment's emergency slush fund is disappearing like water through a sieve." He tapped the pile of reports on his desk. "This has to stop. We can't be wasting resources because one of your deputy chiefs refuses to step down. Harris should take a leave until this Spears business is over. Instead, she's keeping the community in turmoil and using up resources. This is your problem, Dan. You need to get it under control."

Before responding, Dan waited until he'd restrained the blast of fury that hit him square in the chest. It was best that he not lose his temper. A reaction like that wouldn't help anyone. He had a family to support and protect. This was no longer just about him. *Dial it back a notch, Dan.*

"I understand your concerns," he offered as calmly as his anger would allow. "I'll sit down with the comptroller and go through the numbers again to be certain there's no misunderstanding. If I'm wrong about the standing of the department's budget, I'll get things in line." He took a breath, gave himself a mental pat on the back for keeping his voice down and his tone amiable.

Pratt shook his head. "What's happened to you, Dan? We've worked together in one capacity or the other for going on twenty years. You've always been a team player. A man for the people. You know how to get things done and keep the community safe and happy." He shook his head. "Suddenly, it feels like you're an island. No longer a part of all we've built together."

Dan saw red. The outrage tried to gain a foothold once more but Dan held it back. "I'm not operating any differently, Joe. The difference I see is your continued attempts to manipulate my office and my department. I work for the people of Birmingham. Their safety is my top priority. Can you still say the same?"

Before Pratt could stop babbling and say something intelligent and clever, Dan held up a hand. "No need to answer that question. I'm well aware of who you serve. I'm also aware of your hand in the troubles I'm currently experiencing. Mark my word, Joe, I'm not going down without a fight."

"Is that a threat?"

Dan shook his head. "No. It's a promise. I've looked the other way too many times." Dan stood. "Keep holding my feet to the fire and I'm going to do what I should have done years ago. I'll see that you retire far sooner than you had planned."

Dan walked out of the mayor's office without looking back. He'd had enough of the man's games.

To walk off some steam, he chose the stairs rather than the elevator. He shouldn't have allowed Pratt to get so far under his skin, but Dan had remained flexible and reasonable for as long as he could. His patience had thinned to the point of snapping. He didn't intend to make excuses for the mayor's decisions any longer.

The sound of sobbing stopped him midway between the second floor and the first. Was someone hurt? He moved down another tread or two. Definitely a female sobbing. As he descended the final few steps, he spotted the woman standing near the exit. She had her back turned to him. Apparently, on her way out of the building, she had paused near the door to take or make a call.

"No." She shook her head. "That's out of the question." Her voice shook with emotion. "I have to go." She ended the call and reached for the door.

A frown worked its way across Dan's brow as he analyzed the voice. Recognition dawned. "Meredith?"

Meredith Dority jumped and whirled around to face him. "Dan?" The word was barely a croak after all that sobbing.

"Are you all right?" He moved toward her. He hadn't seen Meredith in years. She'd relocated to Montgomery to take a position on the governor's staff. When she'd been Pratt's assistant, they'd had a relationship, and a snap wedding at city hall. The marriage ended with them still friends about a year later. "How long has it been?" At least five years. She'd left with higher aspirations just before he became chief of police. He smiled. "It's good to see you."

"I…" She moistened her lips. "I really have to go."

"Are you okay? Is there anything I can do?"

She shook her head, more tears shining in her eyes. "I'm afraid there's nothing anyone can do." She backed toward the door. "I have to go. I'm… I'm sorry, Dan."

She was out the door before he could get another word out. He had no clue what had happened to upset her so or why she was even in Birmingham.

Another realization dawned. Her mother. "Jesus Christ." Meredith was an only child. Her mother still lived in Birmingham. It was possible her mother had fallen ill or worse. Damn. He threaded a hand through his hair. He should make a call to inquire about Mrs. Dority.

His cell vibrated as he reached for it. Pushing through the door into the steamy afternoon, he checked the screen. Harold Black. *What now?*

"What've you got, Harold?" Black was working the Allen investigation as well as coordinating with the FBI on the Spears investigation. Unless Allen had been found alive and Spears was dead, this would no doubt be unfortunate news.

"We have a development in the Allen case, Dan. Can you meet me in your office ASAP?"

"I'm on my way."

"And Dan."

"Yeah." He hesitated. It seemed life was intent on testing his patience today.

"This needs to stay between us."

The call ended and Dan stared at the screen for a long moment before climbing into his SUV.

When would this nightmare end?

# CHAPTER FOURTEEN

SCOTTSBORO MENTAL HEALTH
CENTER, 12:50 P.M.

"I appreciate you making time to see me, Dr. Thornton." He was younger than Jess had expected. Late thirties, maybe. He was also rather proud of himself.

Every wall was covered with certificates of appreciation from the community for one thing or another. He'd graduated from the University of Alabama in Birmingham. He had a wife, two kids and one dog, based on the framed photo on his desk. What he didn't have was a high regard for law enforcement. His attitude was one of cold indifference. The good doctor evidently had forgotten that Scottsboro was called the Friendly City.

"As I told your detective on the phone," Thornton sent a pointed look at Lori as he leaned back in his chair and clasped his hands over his waist, "I'm not sure what you expect me to say. Doctor-patient privilege prevents me from discussing Amanda Brownfield's case."

"You're absolutely right about that, sir." Jess reached for her bag as if preparing to go. "But, there's this one little exception to that privilege. Maybe you forgot." She fished for her pad and pencil. "You see, Dr. Thornton, you also have an obligation to inform the police if you think your patient is a risk to a third party." Jess smiled sweetly at his taken aback expression. "I'm certain you're familiar with the Tarasoff case of 1976. What we have here, sir, is a similar situation. Amanda's mother has been murdered. Amanda is a suspect for reasons I can't disclose. The trouble that involves you is that there's a strong possibility her boyfriend, Brock Clements, is in grave danger. If anything in your file can help us find Amanda before she harms that man, you have an obligation to tell me. Right now," Jess added for good measure.

"Your point is valid, Chief." Thornton turned his hands up as if her warnings were of little consequence to him. "Get a court order and I'll be happy to assist." He tapped the thick folder on his desk. "I do not intend to have my reputation come into question or to lose my license because the police cannot solve their case. Do your job and I'll do mine. That's my motto."

Now he'd just plain old pissed her off. "I certainly would hate to see Clements' mother sue you if her son is murdered. I feel confident that kind of litigation wouldn't help your reputation, Doctor. If we find her son murdered, I won't have any choice but to tell her about this conversation." Jess frowned with feigned regret. "I hear lawsuits can really jack up those malpractice insurance rates."

Thornton stared at her for a minute, his agitation palpable. "I really don't have time to debate judicial proceedings with you, Chief Harris. I worked you in between patients. Now." He stood. "If you'll forgive me, I have a patient waiting." He opened the folder on his desk. "I'm sure your time is limited as well, I suggest you see yourselves out."

When the door had closed behind him, Jess turned to Lori. "I believe that was an invitation to have a look at the file."

"Sounded like one to me," Lori agreed.

Jess went around the left side of the doctor's desk while Lori skirted the right. Amanda Brownfield's case file was open to the beginning. They quickly skimmed the doctor's reports from his most recent sessions with Amanda.

Several items jumped out at Jess. Delusions of grandeur. Violent episodes. Self-harm. Endless talk of killing. Sexual fantasies about serial killers.

Lori tapped the latest report. "He started her on a stronger drug."

"She must not have responded to the other anti-psychotics he tried," Jess noted. The one listed was a powerful medication with potentially lethal side effects. "There's always the possibility she isn't taking them at all." The file contained photos of Amanda's self-imposed injuries, mostly cutting.

Considering this woman was little Maddie's mother, there was no telling what the child had seen and suffered already. The grandmother had probably taken care of the child more than the mother had. Problem was the grandmother was dead. That didn't leave Maddie with a lot of options

Jess closed the file. "We need to find Amanda Brownfield before anyone else dies." And before she decided she wanted her kid back.

"The boyfriend could be dead already."

"Since we've had no hits on either of their vehicles and no one has seen them since Saturday, you could be right." In Jess's opinion, the odds were against the boyfriend.

"If he knows she killed her mother, he may be looking for a way out."

"Maybe we can help him find it," Jess offered. "If he's still alive." She headed for the door. "Before we move on to the next name on that list the sheriff gave us, let's pay a visit to Clements' mother. Maybe she can shed some light on where the two might be hiding out."

Jess knew one thing: Brock Clements was either a murderer or he'd been murdered.

WOODS COVE ROAD, 2:22 P.M.

Donna Sue Clements lived in a small two-bedroom cottage in a Scottsboro Housing Authority neighborhood near the Jackson County Hospital. Her home was neat and clean and smelled of the pot roast slow cooking in the crockpot for supper. Jess's stomach reminded her that she had skipped lunch. Not a smart thing for a pregnant woman to do. Maybe after this meeting, they could grab a burger.

"He hasn't been home since Saturday," Mrs. Clements said in answer to Jess's question about when she'd last seen her son. "He don't usually go this long without coming home or calling. That's why I went over there looking for him." Perched on the edge of the sofa, she wrung her hands. "You don't think that crazy woman has done something to him, do you? I can't believe she killed her own mother. It's awful, just awful."

"We don't have any evidence to suggest your son has been harmed." Jess saw no reason to mention it was a strong possibility. "We're hoping to find Brock so we can ask him a few questions about Amanda. He's not in any trouble right now."

"I told him she was crazy. Her own momma told me she'd killed ever' cat and dog they'd ever owned. Got'em buried all over the backyard." She shook a finger at Jess. "It was a sad day when Amanda Brownfield had that little girl. Poor child, to have a crazy momma like that. It's just terrible. I hope the law can do something to protect her now that Margaret's gone."

"We'll see that Maddie is well cared for. No need for you to worry about that, Mrs. Clements," Jess assured her. "When you say, Amanda killed all those dogs and cats, was this something she did on purpose or did she just forget to feed them or something like that?"

Clements moved her head from side to side, her expression grave. "Margaret found cats hanging in the barn. Dogs buried alive. After about the fourth time Margaret refused to allow any more pets. The others she killed were strays that had the bad luck of wandering onto the Brownfield farm. We all want to believe the best about our kids, but Margaret knew Amanda was the devil's spawn. She was afraid of her. Run her off years ago but when she come back with that little girl in tow, Margaret couldn't turn her away."

"Do you know what happened to Amanda's father?" Jess's instincts were warning her that the car hidden in the barn was evidence of some sort of foul play.

The older woman harrumphed. "Probably got scared off by Margaret's daddy. Carlton Brownfield was a mean old bastard. He's the reason Margaret didn't have a man in her life until she was past thirty. He scared off any man who dared look at his daughter, much less come calling." Clements nodded knowingly. "For some reason or another he liked Lawrence."

"So Brownfield was Margaret's maiden name?" The Caddy in the barn was registered to a Lawrence Howard. "She never took her husband's name?"

"She and Lawrence never married." Clements shrugged. "I figured her daddy wouldn't allow it even if he did seem to like Lawrence. I always wondered if it was because of Amanda. Margaret and Lawrence kept their relationship secret until she couldn't hide the pregnancy any longer. It was a real strange situation."

DEBRA WEBB

"Do you remember when Lawrence disappeared?" The car was at least three decades old. The question was, if he left of his own volition, why didn't he take it with him? Did he have a second car? Margaret Brownfield's home suggested she lived frugally. Why not sell the car?

"Years and years ago," Clements said. "I guess Amanda was about six. It was real hard on her. She worshipped her daddy. I think that's when she started going crazy. Seemed like his walking out on them done something to her. She wasn't the same after he left."

Abandonment would certainly change a child, though Jess wasn't ready to extend any sympathy to Amanda Brownfield yet. "Did Margaret ever mention hearing from him after that?"

Clements shook her head. "Nope. She wouldn't talk about him at all after he left. Best I can recall, she never mentioned his name again."

"It sounds as if you and Margaret were very good friends, is that correct?"

"When the kids were little. They played all the time. Just like brother and sister but when Amanda got about thirteen, she was always doing something mean to Brock so we stopped going over there. I'd see them in church once in a while but that was a long time ago. When he got mixed up with her again, I reminded him of all them times she hurt him as a kid. He says I don't understand Amanda."

"What sort of things did she do?" Thornton had stated in one of his reports that Amanda Brownfield showed the classic traits of a psychopath. She was likely far more dangerous than this woman knew.

"She pushed him out of the hayloft of that old barn for one thing. Broke his arm. She swore it was an accident, but I knew better even if Brock wouldn't say. She'd take him way out in the woods, tie him up, and then swear she didn't know where he was. God must've been looking out for my boy since he always managed to get loose. Once she tried to bury him. She told him they were playing graveyard. She tried to cover his face with dirt and when he bucked up about it, she hit him in the head with the shovel. He did tell on her for that one. I put my foot down then. Poor Margaret was really upset, but I had to do what was right for my boy." She sighed a weary sound. "But there's only so much a mother can do to protect her child.

Those words weighed heavily on Jess's shoulders. How would she protect her child? "I appreciate your help, Mrs. Clements." Jess passed her a card. "Please call me if you hear from your son."

"I hope you find that crazy gal," Clements said as she followed Jess and Lori to the door. "She should've been locked up a long time ago."

BROWNFIELD FARM, 4:00 P.M.

Gina Coleman and her cameraman had headed back to Birmingham by the time Jess and Lori returned to the farm. Jess didn't blame her, it had been a long day. The search of the barn and the house hadn't turned up any new evidence. Jackson County's evidence tech had worked alongside the two from Birmingham all day. Sylvia had called to tell Jess she'd had a look at Margaret Brownfield's body and concurred with asphyxiation as cause of death. She had suggested further tests to ensure the woman hadn't been drugged which would explain why there was no indication of a struggle. Even the heaviest sleeper typically awakened if they couldn't breathe.

Harper walked Jess and Lori through all the ground he'd covered. Cook was going over the interior of the barn one last time. The yard only went a hundred or so feet all the way around the house before giving way to a pasture on one side, the road on another, and woods on the remaining two.

Jess stopped. "Where's Hayes?" He was supposed to be with Harper and Cook. Had he returned to Birmingham already?

Harper shrugged. "Cook and I had this covered. Hayes wanted to talk to some of the neighbors. He felt hanging around here was a waste of assets."

"He didn't *feel* the need to check with me first?" Ire started to build. Jess liked Hayes, but he needed to understand who was in charge. He might outrank Harper, but as far as Jess was concerned, Harper was senior on this team. When she would have said as much, Hayes appeared around the corner of the house. "Thank you, Sergeant. You and Detective Wells carry on. I need to have a word with the lieutenant."

Tamping down her anger, Jess marched up to Hayes. "We need to take a walk, Lieutenant."

"Yes, ma'am."

Since Jess hadn't been beyond the clearing, she chose one of the numerous trails that went off into the woods. No need for anyone else to hear what she was about to say. When they were deep enough into the woods, she turned on Hayes. "Why did you disobey my orders?" This was not going to fly. The man had a hell of a cocky attitude. It was time she yanked him down a notch or two.

"Harper and Cook had things under control." He executed one of those male, I-don't-know-why-you're-nagging shrugs. "I felt my time could be better utilized checking in with neighbors."

"Did you learn anything useful to this investigation?"

He shook his head. "Afraid not."

After silently counting to five, Jess attempted to speak without shouting. "Moving forward, if you want to remain a member of this team, under no circumstances are you to disobey my orders. Are we clear on that, Lieutenant, or do I need to write it down for you?"

"Crystal clear, Chief."

The rage drained away as abruptly as it had come. Jess suddenly felt more tired than she had in her whole life. She was starving and the M&Ms she carried were gone. That skimpy burger hadn't done anything but make her hungrier. What she needed was a long hot bath and a big of bowl of something hearty and comforting like chicken soup.

"Just don't let it happen again." She dropped her hands to her side. "We're a team. We work together."

"Yes, ma'am."

Whether it was a drop in her blood sugar level or exhaustion, Jess stumbled as she turned to head back to the house. She caught herself, but not before staggering a step or two off the path into the underbrush. Hayes reached for her but it was too late. She went down on her butt. Her bag flew off her shoulder and the contents went flying in every direction.

"Dammit," she snapped.

"You okay, Chief?" Hayes parted the bushes and crouched down next to her.

"Yeah, yeah. I'm fine." After dressing him down, she'd intended to make an impressive exit and look how well that turned out. "My glasses and my phone are in the bushes somewhere." She moved onto her hands and knees and started searching through the undergrowth.

Hayes found her phone and passed it to her.

She spotted her eyeglass case and reached for it. Her fingers grazed something that felt stiff and definitely out of place. She parted the brush, most of which appeared to be dying branches and piles of leaves. The brush scratched at her face but she didn't retreat. The ground felt softer beneath what she now realized was nothing more than a pile of discarded limbs and bush trimmings.

Then she saw what didn't belong.

Fingers... sticking up from the ground.

5 : 0 1 P . M .

Brock Clements was dead. It had taken only a few minutes for Harper and the lieutenant to uncover his body. His body had been too close to the surface to use shovels. Digging by hand, the detectives had worn out three pairs of gloves each.

The Jackson County coroner had arrived. Jess didn't need a coroner or a forensic expert to tell her what happened. Clements had a gash on the back of his head that suggested he'd been temporarily disabled, and then buried in this shallow grave. Before he suffocated, he'd awakened but he'd been too far gone and disoriented to dig his way out from under the shallow blanket of dirt.

Jess had called Sheriff Foster so he could make the notification. She regretted this was the news Mrs. Clement would receive. The loss of a child, no matter the age, went against the nature of things. Mrs. Clements had been right to be worried about her son's involvement with Amanda Brownfield.

Brownfield or her accomplice—not that Jess thought she had one—had done a stellar job of camouflaging the grave. She'd basically replanted some of the brush she dug up right on top of her boyfriend. The recent rain had prevented the leaves from wilting as quickly as they normally would have this time of year. All the shade from the trees had helped as well. The time the killer had spent doing the deed was also marked by the number of cigarette butts left behind.

Rather than watch the body removal, Jess went inside and considered the wall displaying all those photos and newspaper articles. She didn't know how long she'd been inside before Lori came in search of her.

"You ready to call it a day?"

Jess turned to Lori. "Do you think she created this to remind her of some goal?"

Lori nodded. "I think so. Like buying a dress two sizes too small so you don't forget why you're struggling to lose a few pounds."

Jess scanned the wall once more. "Doesn't make sense she'd want to be me. She doesn't even know me." Jess stilled. "Unless it's because Spears is paying attention to me. Maybe that's the attraction."

"He's obsessed with you," Lori reminded her. "Totally obsessed."

Jess considered the disturbing collage. "Amanda could be envious."

"Or she's following his orders," Lori proposed.

"We're coming back tomorrow." Jess gave the room a final once over. "I want to take this place apart piece by piece until we find the answers we need."

# CHAPTER FIFTEEN

Jess tossed her bag onto the sofa and toed off her sneakers. It was good to be home even if the place did smell like the pizza the girls had brought over last night. The odor didn't help her mood. She was dead tired and couldn't decide if the taco she'd eaten on the way home was going to stay down. Lil had called her twice since five o'clock. The first time had been to inquire whether Jess had heard her test results, she had not, and the last time to invite her and Dan to dinner. Meanwhile, Dan had called to say he would be late again.

Jess was too worn out to be good company to anyone. She just wanted to close out the world and relax—if she could stop worrying about Dan. Something was going on with him and he wasn't sharing. Working the case in Scottsboro, Jess felt completely disconnected with what was happening around here. Even the efforts to find Spears had fallen off her radar beyond the possibility that he was somehow involved with Amanda Brownfield. Part of

157

her felt guilty allowing a few hours to go by without thinking of Rory Stinnett and Monica Atmore. The reality was she could do little or nothing for those women. If the Joint Task Force working the Spears case couldn't, how could Jess hope to? She told herself repeatedly that her job was to focus on her case, and still she felt guilty.

"A lifetime of therapy wouldn't fix that, Jess," she muttered.

When Dan came home, she wanted an update on what was going on with him and the Allen case. He wasn't pulling that let's-not-talk-about-work tactic again tonight.

She armed the security system, locked up, and headed for the bathroom. A long hot bath was calling her name. She gathered a fresh towel and her favorite bath oil and placed them next to the tub. When she reached for the razor on the sink, she knocked it to the floor instead.

"Shoot." On her knees, she reached between the toilet and the sink to retrieve the damned thing. That confounded hole she'd meant to patch caught her eye. She hissed a curse. "I'm going to fix you."

Razor in hand, she sat back on her heels and contemplated going next door to ask for caulk. George shouldn't be in bed this early. The hole didn't really worry her. The apartment had been gone over by a top security expert who had found no hidden cameras or listening devices.

Still, bugs and spiders could crawl through holes that size with ease. Her landlord would have already fixed it, if she'd remembered to mention it to him. It wasn't a big deal. She could take care of it. All she needed was a little caulk.

Maybe she'd ask him tomorrow. "No." She pushed to her feet. There was a truckload of things she'd put off already, like getting new clothes and deciding what she and Dan were going to do next about a house and a wedding and...

She groaned. It was time to stop procrastinating. This child would need a home when he or she arrived. Jess had no idea how long it took to build a house, but what she did know was that there was no time to waste.

She marched back to the door, pulled on her shoes, tucked her Glock into her waistband, and went through the paces to open the door. As she descended the stairs, she waved to her surveillance detail. It would be dark soon. Summer was fading fast. Too bad the heat was moving out a whole lot slower. Jess could hardly believe that Labor Day was this coming Monday. Where had the time gone? The invitation to the Baron family barbecue flitted through her head but she wasn't worrying about that right now.

The lights beyond the front windows of her landlord's home glowed. Good, he was still up. She knocked on the door and blinked away the images of the Man in the Moon forcing her out this same door. He'd had a gun to her back and the child he'd abducted in one arm.

Thankfully, that child had survived unharmed and so had Jess. She hoped Maddie Brownfield would come out of this a survivor. That little girl had so many strikes against her already.

The door opened and George Louis smiled. "Jess!" He nudged his glasses up the bridge of his nose. "Come in." Drawing the door open wide in welcome, he asked, "Have you had dinner? I just finished a bowl of the very best stew you've ever eaten."

Jess stepped inside so he could close the door and stop letting all the nice cool air escape. "I had a taco on the way home." Her stomach rumbled defiantly as a hunger pain warned that the nausea had passed and something more substantial was in order. How had she turned into an eating machine so quickly?

"You have to try this stew." He wrapped her arm around his and ushered her into the kitchen. "My sister used to make it on cold winter nights. I decided there was no need to wait for winter to enjoy a good stew."

"Don't go to any trouble for me. I just came over to get some caulk." The aroma of home cooked stew lingered in the air and Jess couldn't deny her mouth was watering.

George frowned as he ladled stew into a bowl. "White caulk?"

"There's a hole in the bathroom floor near the toilet. White would be fine."

"Ah." He nodded. "I guess the electrician who hung the new lights in my garage last year was a little careless with his drill." George set the bowl on the table and motioned for her to have a seat. "We'll get you a little caulk from the garage after you've eaten. Dan isn't home yet?"

Jess was always taking advantage of her landlord's generosity. She hadn't meant to be a bother. "He'll be home later."

George clasped his hands in front of him as if he intended to pray. "We'll send a bowl home for him." He sat down across the table from Jess. "I took a bowl out to the nice young officer watching over you." His face beamed with pride. "He gobbled it right up."

Jess had a taste and she understood why anyone would gobble it up. "This is divine." She had yet to eat anything George prepared that wasn't scrumptious.

He blushed at the compliment. "How is your case going?" His expression turned to one of regret. "I saw that story about you and that evil serial killer. I wish you had told me the sort of trouble you were facing. I could have been watching more carefully."

Someone had been in Jess's apartment at least once. Maybe George was right. An extra level of security never hurt and he was always home. "You probably would have had second thoughts about renting to me if you'd known how often my work followed me home." Her presence in George Louis's garage apartment had certainly been an inconvenience for the man at times. Like when a killer showed up at his door with the child he'd abducted. Or when George had graciously submitted to a thorough search of his property. He had been very accommodating through it all.

"Nonsense." George waved off the suggestion. "I'm very glad you're here. I didn't realize how lonely I'd been until you came into my life." His smile broadened into a big grin. "You keep life interesting."

Jess laughed. "I'm glad you can still see it that way, George."

The conversation turned to football and the upcoming holiday weekend. Since George had no family, he had his own private cookout planned. Jess would have to stop in to say hello—if she wasn't tied up with a case.

That wall of envy Amanda Brownfield had created intruded into Jess's thoughts. Maybe Wanda Newsom was more right than she realized. Jess apparently did have a way of attracting evil.

The thought made Jess angry with herself. Her aunt knew nothing about her life. She was a bitter, lonely old woman desperate for attention. Her conspiracy theories about Jess's father were likely nothing more than the remembered delusions of a former drug addict.

Later, with a hefty bowl of stew wrapped in foil and held in both hands, Jess returned to her apartment. She deposited the stew on the table before going down to the garage to join George in the search for caulk. That big El Dorado she'd yet to see him drive was as clean and shiny as if he'd washed and waxed it today. Every shelf in the garage was neat and organized. The space smelled of wood shavings and oil. Not the kind of oil used in the maintenance of cars but the type furniture refinishers used. George was quite the handyman.

He pointed up to the ceiling. "That's your bathroom. I can't see the hole. Does it come all the way through?"

Jess shrugged. "I don't know. Both times I checked I couldn't see anything, but the light down here wasn't on either of those times so I really can't say."

George retrieved a caulk gun loaded with a tube of the white stuff. "Hold out your hand." Jess turned her left palm up. He squeezed a dollop of the caulk there. "Just stuff that into the hole and wipe away the excess. If that doesn't take care of it, I'll get some tile grout."

"Thanks. I'll do it right now."

George walked her to the bottom of the stairs that led up to her apartment. She thanked him again for dinner then headed up. Hopefully, Dan would be home soon. Until then, that bath was calling her name. She was beyond exhausted. Maybe she should hire George to have dinner prepared every night. She laughed at the idea of how much Dan would love that. He was a damned good cook himself and more than a little skeptical of George Louis.

The caulk worked like a charm and was barely noticeable. Jess rubbed the remainder onto a paper towel and tossed it in the trash. The small can in her kitchen was at the overflow point. Between the pizza box on the floor next to it and the empty wine bottle Sylvia had left, it was past time that the trash was taken out. She thought about waiting until Dan came home, but there was no way to know when that would be and he would be exhausted as well. The sooner she disposed of the box the more quickly the smell would dissipate.

Besides, the exercise would be good for her. At the rate she was consuming whatever anyone put in front of her, she should take advantage of every opportunity to burn a few extra calories.

Glock in her waistband, she descended the stairs once more, waved again to the officer leaning against his cruiser, and headed for the big trash receptacle on the other side of the garage. George's interior lights were out now. The man went to bed with the chickens and was up at the crack of dawn.

Jess lifted the lid and tossed in her bag. It bounced against a discarded box. The logo caught her attention before she tossed the pizza container in. *Babies R Us?* Jess reached in and turned the box over. The shipping label showed George's name and address. Since he didn't have any family, she couldn't imagine what he would be ordering from a store that specialized in baby stuff. She was the one who needed to be shopping there.

"Weird," she muttered as she pitched in the pizza box and let the lid drop. She turned around and ran smack into a body. The air evacuated her lungs before her brain assimilated what her eyes saw. *George.*

"I didn't mean to startle you." He held up a trash bag. "I guess we're on the same wave length.

I wanted to get the trash out of the house before I went to bed."

Jess pressed a hand to her chest. "Jesus." She worked at catching her breath. "You scared the daylights out of me."

He moved around her and dropped his bag into the receptacle. "I'm so sorry. I wasn't trying to sneak up on you. I guess you were distracted."

"Just tired," she assured him, feeling foolish for overreacting. "It's been a strange week."

He patted her arm. "You work too hard, Jess. You need to take some time off. Perhaps you need a hobby. I'm already putting together my Christmas donation for the Children's Charity. I give loads and loads of toys every year."

Her tension eased a bit. "I'd love to help. Please let me know what I need to do."

He ducked his head. "That would mean a great deal to me and to the children."

All the way back to her door Jess felt like a total heel for being suspicious of the old man. He had gone out of his way to be nice to her and she was constantly looking for something wrong. Hazard of the job. Dan's misgivings didn't help either.

Back in her apartment, she locked up, set the alarm, and started that bath she'd been yearning for. She located her favorite nightshirt and something silky and sexy to wear underneath for Dan. As fast as she could, she stripped off her clothes and climbed into the welcoming warmth of the water.

It took a few minutes, but the stress of the day slowly melted from her muscles. She let her mind wander off into the future when she and Dan would have a home of their own and this kid running about. They'd need someone they could trust to take care of the baby. Maybe she'd talk to Lil. She was a nurse. She hadn't worked in years, but now that her kids were away in college she was complaining that she wanted something to do. Maybe Jess would test the waters to see if Lil was interested in being a full time auntie. As far as houses went, the kind and size didn't really matter to Jess as long as Dan was there.

Sleep had just about lured her into its depths when the security system warned that someone was coming up the stairs. She sat up, the water sloshing, and reached for the Glock on the floor next to the tub. Her wet fingers closed around the butt as she listened for footsteps. The sound of the door to her apartment opening had her holding breath.

"Jess?"

*Dan.*

She relaxed and settled the Glock back on the floor. "In here!"

He filled the doorway, took a long look at her and then one of those sexy smiles of his slid across his mouth. Those dimples had her heart doing a little pitty-pat. He stared at her with such longing that it almost took her breath all over again.

"How was your day?" He slipped off his jacket and let it drop to the floor.

She stared at the discarded garment for a moment. "We found another body." She looked up as he came a step closer and reached for the buttons at his cuffs. Every move he made had her heart pounding a little harder.

"I heard." He rolled up first one sleeve and then the other. "The boyfriend?"

Jess nodded, not sure she could speak without stuttering. They were supposed to talk, she reminded herself, but when he knelt next to the tub that thought vanished.

"I'm sorry I'm late again."

He was late. She licked her lips and took one last stab at having that talk with him. "Is something going on you should be telling me about?"

He swept a wisp of hair back from her forehead and then traced the line of her jaw. She shivered. "Not really. Have I told you lately how beautiful you are?" The other hand slipped beneath the water and found her breast. "Still tender?"

That was one of the other things about being pregnant. Her breasts were achy. "Yes. And yes." But the gentle way he touched her made her forget all about aches and pains and weariness. She just wanted him to keep doing it.

His hand slid down her torso, parted her thighs, and started an intimate exploration. "I want you," he murmured.

Her body responded instantly. "Not as much as I want you."

His hand fell away as he stood. Her breath hitched. From this angle, she could clearly see just how much he wanted her. He stripped off his shirt, then his trousers. The socks hit the floor, followed immediately by his boxers.

The water churned and splashed, a little spilling over onto the floor as he settled in the other end of the claw foot tub. He reached for her and she climbed onto him, her legs coming to rest on either side of his waist. While his hands traced her body, her fingers found that part of him she wanted deep inside her. She eased downward, taking all of him before wilting helplessly against his chest.

She closed her eyes and listened to his heart beating. For a long while that was all she needed, just that sound and the feel of him joined with her. His hands tightened around her hips and gently rocked her back and forth. Need ignited, urging her to move faster. She refused. Instead, arching upright, she closed her fingers around the edges of the tub as she set a painfully slow, easy pace.

He taunted her breasts as she teased him with her slow, slow movements. Just watching his face almost undid her. Finally, she closed her eyes and started to glide against him faster and faster until they were plunged into that exquisite place where nothing else mattered.

Just this moment…

# CHAPTER SIXTEEN

Nicole Green's home looked like any other on the block. Two-story brick colonial with a well-manicured lawn and a minivan in the drive. To passersby the multitude of blooming shrubs and colorful toys lying about were nothing more than the expected characteristics of a Mott Street home. It was a family neighborhood where everyone looked out for everyone else.

The kind of neighborhood where people wanted to raise their children. The best public schools in the city. Little or no crime. The closest thing to paradise one found in a city once labeled the murder capital of the country.

But the Green home was no typical family home. It was a safe house used by the Birmingham Police Department on those rare occasions when a victim was in danger and needed the kind of protection found only in a deep cover situation.

"She's eating and sleeping like any other normal four year old," Nicole Green explained to Jess as they watched Maddie Brownfield through the one-way mirror. The family room in the home was set up with monitoring and a viewing area much like the interview rooms at the department. "But that's as far as her normal goes. She doesn't play with the other children. She doesn't speak to anyone. She watches and she draws."

Jess turned to the other woman. "Watches?"

Nicole, a nurse practitioner with a specialty in pediatric psychology, hesitated before answering as if she needed to find the right way to answer. "I'm hesitant to label her behavior. It's too soon. But if I had to give my impressions to a judge today, I'd say she has spent most of her life very sheltered."

An uneasy feeling crept up Jess's spine. "Define sheltered."

"No social interaction with other children." Her eyebrows reared up in skepticism. "Maybe no social interaction with anyone beyond her immediate family. She doesn't speak. She appears confused when the other children try to play with her. I think that's why she watches. When she watches long enough to feel comfortable, she imitates what she sees. But mostly, she draws. No matter what's on the television she ignores it. I get the impression she's seen very little television, which, in my opinion, isn't such a bad thing. That may have been the one good thing her caregivers did for her."

The nausea hadn't haunted Jess this week the way it had the last, but right now she felt very sick to her stomach. "I'd like to speak to her if you think it won't interfere with your ongoing assessment."

"Actually," Nicole said, "I'd like to see how she reacts to you."

"All right." Jess had spent twenty years working in law enforcement and this case, this child, or maybe her pregnancy, had her hesitating. "I'd like to show her photos of her mother, grandmother, and her mother's boyfriend."

Nicole made a face as she contemplated the request. "Do you believe there's something she can tell you that's going to help your investigation?"

Jess shook her head. "I'm not sure she can tell me anything but her reaction might tell me if she was afraid of her mother's boyfriend which could explain why he got himself buried alive."

"I suppose it can't hurt to see how she reacts to the mother and grandmother. If there's no problem you can show her the photo of the boyfriend. Use your own judgment." Nicole shrugged. "Whatever happens is on you, Chief Harris. My job is to protect that little girl."

Now that Jess felt like the bad guy in the room, she squared her shoulders and did what she understood she had to do. "Thank you. I'll bear that in mind."

Jess opened the door and entered the family room. Maddie didn't look up. Her focus remained on her coloring. Jess hiked her tangerine skirt up a few inches and settled on her knees next to the little girl.

"Hello, Maddie."

Maddie looked up at Jess and smiled. Jess's heart squeezed. "What're you drawing today?"

Maddie looked down at the picture in progress. A house and a small stick figure stood amid several trees. Probably the farmhouse. Jess studied the drawing closer. Between the trees were little green hills or… mounds. She pointed to one. "What's this?"

Maddie stared up at Jess as if she didn't understand.

Jess picked up the sheet of craft paper and pointed from one mound to the next. They pretty much filled the page. "Are these flowers? Or shrubs?"

Maddie shook her head.

Jess's throat went dry as she thought of all the murdered animals Mrs. Clements had told her about. "Is something buried here?" She placed her finger on one mound after the other.

Maddie nodded.

Jess moistened her lips. "Can you tell me what it is?"

The little girl curled her finger for Jess to come closer. Jess leaned down.

Maddie put her little face next to Jess's ear and whispered, "The dead people."

Heart bumping against her sternum, Jess summoned a smile for the little girl. "May I keep this one? I would really love to hang it on my wall?"

Maddie nodded and reached for a new page. She returned to her coloring as if the past few seconds hadn't happened.

Jess placed the photos of Amanda and Margaret Brownfield on the floor in front of Maddie. The little girl glanced at them but hardly spared more than a second or two from her drawing. Next, Jess laid Clements' photo in front of her. Maddie looked at him and, once more, returned to her drawing.

"Do you know these people, Maddie?"

This time the child didn't look up, she just kept coloring.

"I'll be back to see you soon, Maddie."

Somehow, Jess left the room without breaking into a run. When the door was closed Nicole asked, "Did she tell you anything that could help?"

"Maybe." Jess couldn't be sure what the child had witnessed or even been forced to participate in. "Until we see what this means," she showed the drawing to Nicole, "you may want to watch her closely with the other children."

Confused, Nicole shook her head. "Is there some implication I'm not seeing?"

"She told me there are dead people buried here. Since we've already found one, I believe her."

Shock claimed the other woman's face. "I'm going to need to speak with Mrs. Wettermark about this."

"If she's moved, I'll need the location," Jess said on her way out. She had calls to make as well.

Clint Hayes waited for her in the entry hall. "We ready, Chief?"

"We are. Have you heard from Dr. Baron yet?"

Hayes went out the door first, surveyed the street, then moved aside for Jess to exit. "She's headed to Scottsboro now to have a look at Clements' body."

"Then that's where we're headed." Jess plucked her sunglasses from her bag and pushed them into place. "Warn Chief Burnett that we're going to need a full forensic team at the Brownfield farm. I'll give Agent Manning a call at the Birmingham Field Office. We may need the body hunters on this one."

"Yes, ma'am."

As Hayes withdrew his cell phone, Jess reached for the passenger side door. It was looking like she'd found another cunning serial killer. She thought of the photos and articles on the wall of Amanda Brownfield's wall. Or had the serial killer found her? Jess shuddered as she dragged her seatbelt into place.

After she and Dan had made love last night, she'd laid in bed listening to him breath. She had spent several hours thinking about Amanda Brownfield before she could sleep. Jess had decided that if her conclusions were correct, the woman fell a little higher on the evil scale than Richard Ellis. Richard had been vicious in his need to assuage the pain of rejection. But Amanda wasn't trying to assuage anything as simple as a rejection. Her methods reached the next level.

She was beyond vicious... Amanda Brownfield was vile.

Jess doubted that Dr. Brazelton had ever encountered anyone in his profession quite like Sylvia Baron. She was unquestionably one of a kind. As usual, she was dressed impeccably. A lime green dress and matching stilettos. The gorgeous shoes made Jess yearn for her lost Mary Janes. Oh well, there would be other shoes.

"Your killer was quite resourceful in her methods," Sylvia announced.

"The gash on the back of his head was sufficient for keeping him down?" Jess studied the victim. Brock Clements had plenty of tattoos like Amanda's other boyfriend. A little less bulk, but still abundantly muscled for such a lean frame. Despite his lack of ambition on the job, he'd been handsome enough. Too bad he hadn't put those looks to better use, namely keeping a job and finding a girlfriend who wasn't a psychopath. She had marked him with her signature red lipstick imprint just as she had her mother. Poor bastard.

"The knock to the head likely rattled him enough for her to get him in the hole she'd dug," Sylvia speculated. "His clothes showed evidence of having been dragged through the dirt and brush.

He could have been rattled long enough for her to cover him up, but then he pulled himself together. Judging by the combination of skin and dirt found under his nails, he may have grabbed her while she was packing down the dirt."

"Did she drug him?"

"No evidence of that so far." Sylvia drew back the sheet to expose more of his torso. "She tased him."

Jess spotted the telltale red marks. "Why not just shoot the guy?" Jess complained. "The end results are the same and without all the hubbub."

"I blame it on all the violence on television and in those disturbing video games," Sylvia tossed back. "Killers these days need more stimulation during the act."

Brazelton just looked from one to the other.

"So the Taser did him in?" Jess asked. All Amanda had needed was to keep him down until he'd suffocated.

"Not the first time." Sylvia lifted his right shoulder and indicated another mark. "But the second one finished the job."

Damn. The guy had to know he was screwed by the time she hit him with that second jolt of electricity. "Not a good way to go."

"At least he had sex one last time before he bit the dust, literally."

Jess smiled, pretending she didn't notice the rush of red up the Jackson County Coroner's face. "Thank you for coming all this way to lend a hand, Dr. Baron."

Sylvia tugged off one glove and then the other. "Anytime, Chief Harris. Don't forget about the barbecue on Monday. My father will be most disappointed if you're not there."

"I wouldn't miss it."

Jess thanked Dr. Brazelton for making this autopsy a priority as she stripped off the protective wear. Lieutenant Hayes hadn't donned the requisite gloves since he had opted not to get close enough to touch the victim. Jess wondered if he honestly had the stomach for investigating murder cases.

"We have a forensic team on site," he told her as they exited the building. "Harper said Agent Manning had arrived. He has an excavation team en route."

"Good. I'd like to know what we're looking at before nightfall. Is Agent Gant with him?" Gant had told Jess he was coming.

"Harper said Gant couldn't make it."

Which meant just one thing. Something higher priority had come up. Jess hoped it was an actual lead on Spears. "Thank you, Lieutenant."

"Harper also said Chief Black called to let you know that homeless guy, Terry Bellamy, hanged himself in his cell last night."

Jess's step faltered. "Are they sure it was suicide?"

"That's what Black says."

Spears had used a young woman to relay a message to Jess once. She too had hung herself. Terry Bellamy had served his purpose and Spears had eliminated that loose end. "Let Black know I'd like to see the case file."

"Will do."

Halfway across the parking lot her cell rang. A Birmingham number but not one she recognized. "Harris."

"Jess Harris?"

Female. Jess's pulse skipped into a faster rhythm. "This is she."

"This is Melissa, Dr. Fortune's nurse."

Jess stopped. "You have the results of my tests back?"

"We do, and the news is good. Dr. Fortune wanted me to pass along that you do not have Wilson's disease and the rest of your labs were normal."

Jess reached for the car to steady herself. Thank God. "Thank you." She ended the call and dropped her phone back into her bag. At least that was one less thing to worry about.

"You all right, Chief?"

The lieutenant studied her from the other side of his car. "As a matter of fact, I'm better than all right, Lieutenant."

For the first time in more than a week, Jess felt like herself. Between the pregnancy and Spears, she'd been a little off balance.

"What now?"

"Now we have a killer to catch."

BROWNFIELD FARM, 4:30 P.M.

"What're we looking for?" Lori surveyed the living room.

"Since there's nothing we can do outside at the moment," Jess tugged on a new pair of latex gloves, "we're going to dig around for any of Amanda's secrets in here."

The excavation team had tagged several locations for digging. The noise outside warned that it had begun.

"Should we start in her room?"

Jess shook her head. "The wall was for us to find. Her real secrets, the ones she doesn't want anyone to see, won't be so easily discovered." Jess moved around the room as she spoke. "She thinks she's smarter than the people she murders. She believes she's far superior to the police. She isn't worried about getting caught. She has just one goal."

"To satisfy the Player?" Lori suggested. "You think she's doing his bidding like the Man in the Moon and Ellis did?"

Jess considered the question a moment. "I think she's trying to impress him. She wants him to be excited by her. To admire her. She doesn't understand he's using her."

Jess had already set Hayes, Cook, and Harper on a similar task in the barn. Whatever secrets Amanda had hidden, Jess intended to find them.

Two hours later, Jess found what they'd been looking for. With the rug moved away from the sofa, the scars on the wood floor showed the sofa had been moved repeatedly. After sliding the sofa eighteen inches from the wall, along the path of the marks on the floor, Jess crouched down to have a look. Lori did the same, moving toward Jess from the other end of the sofa.

Three shorter pieces of wood flooring were loose. A butter knife from the kitchen helped to pry the first board up. The final two popped up easily. There was no subfloor. Since the front of the house was so close to the ground, the floor joists literally touched the earth in this area of the crawlspace. In the cavity between two joists was a metal box. A small one, like an old-fashioned cash box.

Lori reached down and brought it up. She dusted it off and passed it to Jess. Whether it was women's intuition, some sixth sense, or a premonition, things Jess had never believed in, her hands shook as she slid the small lock button that allowed her to open the lid.

Inside were photos and folded papers. Birth certificates. One for Amanda and another for Maddie. This was the first time she'd seen the child's. No father listed. Jess rifled through the photos. All were of men. Dozens and dozens of them. Were they Amanda's boyfriends? Some looked too old, or rather their manner of dress looked too out of date to have been men Amanda would have known.

Jess's fingers stilled on one photo and her heart seemed to do the same. For three beats she couldn't breathe much less speak. Her face must have gone deathly white.

"Do you recognize him?" Lori asked, concern in her voice.

Jess turned to her, swallowed to moisten her throat. "I'm not sure." She felt a little lightheaded. "I think I need a drink of water."

"I'll grab a bottle for you."

When Lori had gone, Jess dragged her bag closer and pulled out her cell. She stared at the photo, her heart thudding in her chest. Her fingers shook as she tapped the screen.

Two rings later Corlew answered. "What's up, kid?"

Jess opened her mouth to speak but the words wouldn't come. She stared at the photo... at the man who was her *father*. "I need to see you as soon as possible."

"I can come over tonight."

She nodded then realized he couldn't see. "'kay."

"Chief!"

*Harper.*

"I have to go." Shaken to the core, Jess shoved the phone into her bag. On second thought, she grabbed an evidence bag for the photo of her father and then stuffed it into her bag as well. The rest she put back into the metal box. "Right here, Sergeant."

Jess got to her feet. Her knees threatened to buckle causing her to grab onto the back of the sofa.

Shock must have been going around because Harper looked a little pale himself.

"You're gonna want to come outside and see this."

Lori walked up behind him. "Oh my God." She glanced back out the door. "What the hell happened here?"

Jess smoothed her skirt and forced her legs to carry her to the door. She surveyed the yard. There were dozens of holes.

"We need to get Sheriff Foster back out there." Harper moved into the huddle with them. "We got remains in every one of those holes."

# CHAPTER SEVENTEEN

Dan stopped his SUV in the street in front of his parents' home. "We can go back home if you're not up to this."

Apparently, her silence had Dan worried that she didn't want to talk to his parents tonight. What Jess really wanted was to talk to Corlew, but Dan had called her at half past five and told her to come home. He'd refused to explain. He'd insisted he needed her to come home. Sensing his desperation, she'd left Harper, Cook, and Hayes at the Brownfield farm. Lori had driven her home. Thankfully, she hadn't asked about the photo. Jess wasn't ready to talk about that to anyone but Corlew... not until she understood what it meant. She also refused to consider that she had taken evidence from the scene.

After the fastest shower on record and still no explanation, she and Dan had come straight here. Jess would have preferred to know what was going on before they arrived at the Burnetts' but, on some level, she'd understood that he wasn't ready to talk.

183

She'd noticed the haunted look in his eyes the past two nights. Something was wrong and he hadn't wanted to talk about it. Now they sat in the middle of the street with this whatever it was hanging between them, and a BPD cruiser right behind them waiting for some sort of indication as to what they were going to do.

"No." Jess broke the silence. "I'm glad we're here. We might as well give them the news. Lil knows and your parents should too." Why not? She had the remains of at least twenty people at the Brownfield farm and the body hunters weren't finished by a long shot. She'd found a photo of a man who was either her father or his twin in a box kept by the murder suspect. It had been a great day! What was one more drama-filled scene before it was over?

"We don't have to do that," Dan argued quietly.

The dim glow of the interior lights didn't allow her to see his face very well and she needed to. Dammit. She needed to know what was going on. "Then why did you call me home from a mass murder scene to come over here and *not* tell them?" Jess laughed. She had to laugh or she was going to cry. "It's not like family night couldn't wait."

"It can't wait."

Fear trickled through her. "Dan, please tell me what's going on." She reached out and touched his jaw, felt the tension there.

"Harold came by to see me this afternoon. He suggested I take a leave of absence until this thing with Allen is straightened out."

"What?" Anger blasted away any fear that had crept in. She wanted to kick something. Maybe Harold Black for starters. "Why would you do that?" She had an idea. Possibly, so Black could slip into the position of chief of police.

"He's trying to help, Jess."

"You can't still believe that." She wanted to shake Dan for continuing to trust the guy. "He's trying to take you down."

"He warned me about the search warrant being issued on the house," he reminded Jess.

"And then your house was virtually destroyed in the fire," she reminded him. "Doesn't that smell like a set up to you? Now he can testify that he told you about the warrant. That makes you look all the guiltier, Dan. Can't you see where this is headed?"

"There's more."

Jess sagged against the seat. There was only one other time in her life that she'd ever heard Daniel Burnett talk like this—with that defeated, I'm-done tone... when he gave up on their relationship, breaking their engagement, and leaving her in Boston all those years ago.

*He was giving up.*

"Fine. Let's hear it." Jess crossed her arms over her chest.

"Pratt is gathering the necessary support to demand my resignation."

Jess scoffed. "Who's surprised about that? He's been angry with you since the day you asked me to come to Birmingham and help with the Murray case." And that was the bottom line. None of this was about Dan. It was about her. She closed her eyes and fought the infuriating sting of tears.

*Damn you, Spears.*

"Harold insisted there were things he couldn't share, but he kept repeating that it would be best for everyone," Dan turned to her, "including you."

"I will not let you do this, Dan, do you hear me?" She couldn't allow this to happen. *No.* She wouldn't allow it. Dammit.

He smiled for her but it was far from his usual charming display. "I love you, you know that, right? I would do anything for you and our baby."

"Then give me time to end this with Spears." She battled with the tears stinging her eyes. "Don't let him get away with this, Dan. He's taken too much already."

"You sure you're prepared to weather the kind of storm Pratt and the people who run this town are prepared to launch against us?"

Laughter swelled in her throat. "I've been butting heads with people like Pratt since I was ten years old, Daniel Burnett. There is absolutely nothing he can do to me that will shake me. I've never given men like him power over me."

"You always were the strong one." He searched her face. "I let you down once, Jess. I won't let you down again."

A fresh wave of tears brimmed. "If we don't go inside, I'm going to embarrass you right here in the street by starting something neither of us will be able to stop. Your mother will be mortified."

He laughed. "All right. Let's go make my mother the happiest woman on the planet."

Jess swallowed back a groan. She couldn't wait.

9:30 P.M.

"That son of mine is working you entirely too hard, Jess." Katherine Burnett's face puckered in feigned concern. "You look so tired."

"Well, I've been digging up dead people all afternoon, Katherine." Jess heaved a sigh as she set her coffee cup aside. "It does get tiring."

Dan's mother put her hand to her chest. "My word." She looked to her husband and then to Dan before turning back to Jess. "Are you working on that case up in Jackson County?"

"I am."

Katherine shook her head. "This is related to that little girl left on the street? I saw her on the news. It's just awful."

"It is. Yes, ma'am." Jess leaned into the sofa and tried for the tenth time to relax. It was never easy around Katherine.

"I don't know what this world is coming to," Dan Senior said with a somber shake of his head.

"I'm right there with you, Dad." Dan set his cup and saucer on the coffee table as well.

Since it had been too late for a proper southern dinner, Katherine had prepared finger foods and a lemon pie. Jess hadn't meant to eat two slices—a fact Katherine would never permit her to forget. They'd retired to the living room with their coffee after dessert. Jess stifled a yawn. Katherine was right about one thing, she was exhausted.

Dan took Jess's hand and cradled it between his. "There may be some trouble brewing at the office."

This was so wrong. Jess would do almost anything to take this weight off his shoulders.

Dan Senior leaned forward and braced his forearms on his knees. "What sort of trouble?"

Katherine sent a suspicious look at Jess. "Is this related to that monster that followed Jess here?"

Dan held Jess's hand a little tighter. He was probably worried she would jump over the coffee table and throttle his mother. She'd gone this long without doing something to his mother she would regret. No need to start now.

"We can't be sure where the trouble is coming from, but I'm being investigated in the disappearance of Ted Allen."

Katherine jumped to her feet. "That's the most ridiculous thing I've ever heard. One of those drug people he was trying to stop probably stopped him first. Why in the world would anyone believe you had anything to do with it?"

"Now, now, Katherine." Dan Senior patted her arm. "Settle down and let the boy finish what he has to say."

As the woman wilted into her seat, Jess couldn't help feeling sorry for her. She was so proud of her son. This was going to hurt.

"Evidence suggesting I was involved has been planted," Dan went on. "I believe the fire at my house is related somehow as well."

Katherine was on her feet again. "You could've been killed!" She blinked and then turned to Jess as if she'd just remembered. "Jessie Lee, too."

Dan Senior didn't bother telling her to sit this time. "This is more serious than you're telling us."

With a heavy breath, Dan nodded. "There's no way to know what's going to happen next, but it may get ugly."

Katherine's eyes rounded. "Will this make the news?"

Dan laughed but the sound held no humor. "I'd say that's a given."

"Oh, good Lord." Katherine swayed.

"Sit down, Katherine," Dan Senior said a bit more firmly. "It hasn't happened yet. Dan's only trying to prepare us for the worst."

"It's her fault!" Katherine pointed an accusing finger at Jess.

Jess stiffened. Considered that she might have to change her mind about doing something she could potentially regret.

Katherine shook that finger. "You did this. You dragged him away from home twenty-four years ago, and now you've come back to ruin him. Why didn't you stay away, Jess? You've never been anything but trouble for Dan."

More times than she could count, Katherine Burnett had said things to Jess that were meant to wound but Jess had always let them go. She'd never cared what the woman thought of her. But somehow, this time she couldn't.

Maybe because this time Katherine was right.

The tears came so swiftly and with such force Jess couldn't hope to hold them back.

The silence that followed was somehow more excruciating than Katherine's words. Why wasn't Dan defending her? When she turned to him, she instinctively recoiled. The look of rage on his face was one she had never seen before. She held her breath. The storm wasn't coming... it had arrived.

"As much as I love you, Mother," Dan said, his voice deceptively calm, "I will not have you speak to Jess that way. If you don't respect her and care for her, then we have a very serious problem."

"Sit down, Katherine," Dan Senior insisted.

"You're going to marry her, aren't you?" Katherine said, her voice quivering. "I have done everything I know to keep you from repeating the mistake that tore you apart all those years ago and you won't listen." Katherine shook her head. "Mark my words, you'll be even sorrier this time than you were the last."

There was a great deal Jess could have said, but this was between Dan and his mother. All she could do was ride it out. She wasn't so much surprised at how Katherine felt. It was more that she was startled the woman would say it out loud with Jess in the room.

Dan stood. Jess rose to stand beside him. She hoped he wouldn't say anything in the heat of the moment that he would regret later. This woman was his mother after all.

"Good night," he announced.

Jess wanted to cheer. Leaving without more hurtful words being exchanged was the right decision. Besides, Jess was so ready to go.

"Son, wait." Dan Senior got to his feet and held out his hands in a placating manner. "Your mother's upset. She doesn't mean any of this." He glared at Katherine. "Do you?"

She said nothing, obviously too overcome to speak at this point. Too bad that couldn't have happened about five minutes ago.

"I love Jess," Dan told his mother. "We're getting married." Katherine's lips trembled. "If we're all going to be a family, then you need to accept that."

Katherine shook her head. "I cannot accept it."

"Good God, Katherine," Dan Senior growled. "You're making a fool of yourself."

Jess held up her hands. She had to stop this. As painful as it was for her, she couldn't bear to watch what it was doing to Dan. "It's all right. We don't have to figure this out tonight."

"You need to apologize, Mother," Dan warned, his face still hard with fury.

Jess shook her head. "No, it's—"

Katherine lifted her chin. "I will not apologize for speaking what's in my heart."

Well, hell. Jess was about ready to walk over and shake the woman. She just wouldn't give it a rest.

"Then I guess you won't mind when we don't allow your grandchild to come over for play dates."

Jess wished she could crawl under a rock.

Uncertainty flashed in Katherine's expression. "Well," she began, "when that time comes—"

"That time has already come," Dan let her know.

Katherine looked puzzled before turning to glare at Jess. "Are you saying she's…?"

"Yes," Dan stated. "Jess and I are having a baby."

Like any true southern bell when faced with life altering news, Katherine fainted.

Dan and his father rushed to Katherine's aid. Jess didn't bother. She was positive Katherine didn't want her help. Suited Jess just fine. The woman had made her feelings perfectly clear. Her news hadn't really been news at all.

Jess's cell rang and she was grateful for the distraction. She fished in her bag until she found it. Gina Coleman's name flashed on the screen.

"You have some news?" Jess moved into the kitchen away from the drama.

"Jess, you need to turn on the television. Channel Three. Where's Dan?"

"We're at his parents'." Jess went to the kitchen island and grabbed the remote lying there. She turned on the set. "What am I looking for?" Fear started a new journey through her.

"I called as soon as I heard there's going to be breaking news about Dan."

Even as Gina said the words, the anchor echoed them. "Dan!" Jess shouted, her heart starting to pound.

"I didn't know this was coming," Gina was saying as Dan and his parents hurried into the kitchen. "I usually get a heads up from one of my sources, but they kept this hush-hush."

A photo of Dan appeared on the screen behind the anchor. "Former mayoral assistant Meredith Dority," a picture of Dan's first wife appeared on the screen next to the one of him, "came forward this evening in an exclusive interview with Channel Three reporter, Gerard Stevens."

Jess's gaze found Dan's. He shook his head. Was this what he'd been distracted with the past two nights?

"According to Dority, Chief of Police Daniel Burnett was instrumental in a number of instances of investigation tampering and witness strong arming in his days as liaison between the mayor's office and the position he now holds. A full investigation has been launched."

A video clip of Pratt rolled. "The city of Birmingham has my solemn promise that these allegations will be fully investigated."

The anchor droned on but Jess didn't hear anymore. She'd heard enough.

Katherine turned to Dan. "Why is Meredith saying those things?"

"I can't answer that question." Dan shook his head. "Until this week, I hadn't seen her in years."

"Her allegations are fabricated," Dan Senior said firmly. "Know that we're behind you, son. I still have friends who will rally support for you."

Jess wished it were that simple. Her cell rang again. She stared numbly at the screen. Corlew. She'd have to call him back.

Katherine hugged her son. "I'm so sorry."

Dan Senior hugged them both. Tears welled in Jess's eyes again. Dan needed their support now more than ever. This was going to get even uglier.

Three weeks ago, Corlew had made some comment about Dan and some fixed cases in the past but Jess refused to believe him. She didn't believe he'd done any such thing before becoming chief of police as Dority was alleging either. Dan Burnett was not capable of such underhandedness. He was far too ethical and honorable.

As if he'd heard her thought, he pulled away from his parents and came to her. He drew Jess into his arms and held her tight. "I wish I could make this go away."

She bit her lip. Tried her best to keep those blasted tears back but it wasn't happening. "We'll get through it."

A tug on her arm had Jess turning from his comforting embrace.

"I was wrong to say all that," Katherine implored. "I'm very happy for you and Dan." Her voice quavered but she got the words out. "The past is the past. It has no place in the present."

Jess rustled up a smile. Those words must have hurt. "Thank you."

The next group hug included Jess. She decided this part was going to take some getting used to.

By the time they loaded into Dan's SUV to go home, Jess felt confident the revelations were over for tonight. She'd heard a few more than she would have preferred but life was like that sometimes.

Dan started the engine but rather than putting the Mercedes into gear he just sat there.

Jess put a hand on his arm. "You okay?"

He looked at her for a long moment before he answered. "I don't want to wait until this insanity is over."

She frowned, tried to read his face. "What do you mean?"

"Let's get married tomorrow. We'll just drive to wherever we want to go and find a judge and do it."

Except she had at least twenty murder victims waiting for justice and a sister who would never forgive her if she and Dan eloped.

Jess patted his arm. "We could do that, but I don't think our families would forgive us in this lifetime. How about we give the idea a little more thought first?"

Dan didn't answer. He just put the SUV in gear and drove away.

And here she'd thought this night couldn't get any more complicated.

# CHAPTER EIGHTEEN

Lori loaded the laundry she'd sorted into the machine and pushed the start button. As the water rushed into the machine, she braced against it and closed her eyes. What was she doing?

How much longer could she keep doing this to Chet?

She'd been avoiding intimacy with him since he told her about the complication that came with the surgery. This wasn't how she'd planned her life. She'd expected to rise high enough in her career to be financially stable with a comfortable savings account before marriage and kids. She'd watched her mother struggle with finances after her father died.

Fury tightened her lips. Unlike her younger sister, who'd been just a toddler when their father killed himself, Lori remembered the man. He'd seemed so solid, so warm and caring. He'd made her laugh and taken care of her when she skinned

196

her knees. She remembered watching him wax the Mustang. He'd wink and tell her it would be hers one day.

"Bastard," she said between clenched teeth. He'd loved them so much he'd taken the easy way out when life got a little hard. He'd left them to fend for themselves. Lori's mother had cleaned houses for Birmingham's elite until she was too old to do the backbreaking work. Lori had made a promise to herself and to her younger sister. They were never going to struggle that way. She had ensured her sister had the necessary funding to go to a good university. She had helped her mother pay off the mortgage on the family home. Now it was her turn to ensure her future was financially stable.

She would not dive into motherhood before she was ready to take care of a child for the long haul. She just couldn't do it.

"Are you that mad at me?"

Lori whirled around at the sound of Chet's voice. He stood in the laundry room doorway watching her. "I thought you were in bed." She wasn't sure she was prepared to have the conversation now. Maybe she never would be.

"I was. But you weren't." He pushed away from the door and closed in on her, trapping her between the washing machine and his body. "I don't have to do the surgery now. We can wait another year or so."

The sad mixture of pain and hurt in his eyes tugged at her heart. All he wanted was for her to be happy… with him. Why couldn't she give him that? He wasn't her father.

"I was just thinking about my dad." The anger she felt at her father twisted into a big knot in her chest. "I loved him so much and he left us. We barely survived." She couldn't look at Chet as the tears glided down her cheeks. She was stronger than this. Dammit all to hell.

"You may never fully understand the reason your father took his life, Lori. I guess I'll never know who murdered mine. But, I'm not your father or mine." She lifted her gaze to his. "I'm the man who loves you more than life itself. I won't have you unhappy and I will never willingly leave you. If this is a problem, we don't need to have children until you're ready. I'm good with that."

She shook her head, scrubbed at the tears. "I just don't want our children to ever struggle. I want us to build a secure life before we go filling it with mouths to feed. I feel like I have an obligation to be prepared before entering into parenthood."

Everything she said seemed to add to the hurt in his eyes. Why couldn't she say the right words?

"I feel the same way. I have a solid savings, Lori. I have an account for Chester's college and a savings account for emergencies and the future. I add to both of those every payday. I'm not some broke guy who doesn't know how to take care of his family."

The hint of hurt and anger in his voice stabbed like a knife. "I know this." She rubbed his arm, gave it a squeeze. "You're a good man, Chet. You've done everything right. I just want to make sure I do my part right."

A grin slid across his lips. "You already took the first step by choosing me."

She laughed. Couldn't help herself. "I guess I did."

"Hell." He shrugged those broad shoulders of his. "For that matter, I can get the surgery done and freeze some sperm until we're ready. That way we don't have to worry about the scar tissue blocking things up. We'll have all the time in the world."

Lori smiled up at him. She was so very blessed to have found this man. "You know what? Sometimes things are just meant to be." She took a big breath and went for it. "Have the surgery. I'll stop taking the pill and whatever happens, happens."

The pain in his eyes vanished, leaving only the hope. "You're sure about this? I don't want you to regret your decision later."

"I will never regret anything I do with you." She looped her arms around his neck. Enjoyed the feel of his bare chest against her.

His arms went around her and he caressed the skin between the closure of her bra and her panties. She felt the press of his desire against her bellybutton. "What changed your mind?" he asked softly.

She traced his mouth with one fingertip, left a kiss on his chin. "Someone I respect very much shared a huge secret with me. She made me realize that you can't control everything."

He captured that fingertip between his teeth and nipped it before inquiring, "Are you allowed to share this secret?"

"Only with you." She made him wait for a few seconds then she couldn't take it anymore. "Jess is pregnant."

"What?" He looked as stunned as Lori had been.

"With all that's going on, she missed a couple of pills and she just learned she's pregnant."

"Oh man." Chet shook his head. "With Burnett's house pretty much destroyed, this Spears shit, and the trouble he's having with the Allen case, no wonder they're both so stressed out. What're they going to do?"

Lori shrugged. "We didn't go into that but I think they'll get married. They're crazy in love with each other."

"So this changed your mind?"

Lori shook her head. "No. But it made me see that life is not something you can plan down to the moment. It happens. You try your best to be prepared for whatever life brings, but the one thing you can't do as long as you're breathing is stop it from happening." She searched Chet's eyes. Hoped her words conveyed how very much she wanted to be with him and to have his children. "I don't want to stop *us* from happening. I want to relish every moment of life with you no matter what it brings. We'll deal with each new development just like we do in the cases we investigate."

His smile was so sweet, so tender, that tears stung her eyes once more. "You are the most amazing woman, Lori Wells. I want to spend the rest of my life making you the happiest woman in the world."

She stilled, her heart threatening to burst from her chest. "Did I hear you wrong or did you just propose to me?"

"You just now noticing?" He leaned down and kissed her lips. "I've been trying to get you to marry me for weeks."

She held up her left hand and wiggled her fingers. "Then you better put a ring on it, mister."

"In that case." He took her by the hand and led her through the house to the bedroom. He ushered her to the bed. "Sit right there."

"You know," she said as she sat on the edge of the bed and he went into the walk-in closet, "I didn't picture this with you in your boxers." Her heart was racing so hard she could hardly breathe. Was this really happening? She couldn't believe it!

Chet returned, his hands behind his back. "Like you said, life happens." He got down on one knee in front of her.

She gasped, fresh tears brimming on her lashes. "Chet, this is... crazy. Are you sure about this?"

"Lori," he presented a velvet box and opened it, "will you do me the honor of becoming my wife?"

She stared at the ring. It was a beautiful square cut diamond that was much bigger than she'd ever expected. "You shouldn't have spent so much money!"

He gave her a pointed look. "Is that a yes?"

She choked out a laugh. "Yes." She sighed, her lips trembling. "Yes, Chet Harper, I will be your wife."

He took the ring from the box, slid it onto her finger, and then he kissed her. "I love you."

She smiled, her lips brushing his. "I love you."

They climbed onto the bed and made love. His every move was so tender and sweet Lori thought she might die before they came together. The moment was perfect. The ring was perfect. *He* was perfect.

For a long time they lay in each other's arms, enjoying the incredible afterglow of their lovemaking. When work slipped into her thoughts, Lori felt guilty. She hoped he didn't feel the new tension growing inside her. She was worried about not only this case but Jess and the chief.

"This is the worst crime scene of my career," Chet murmured.

She bopped him on the chest. "I was feeling guilty even thinking about work."

He laughed. She loved that deep sexy sound. "We have twenty or so sets of remains. It's kind of hard not to think about it."

"At least it's not children like all those kids the Man in the Moon murdered." Murder was murder but when it was a child… Lori shuddered.

Chet hugged her tighter. "Yeah, that was rough."

Lori thought about the other discovery she and Jess had made. "You know that metal box Jess found?"

"Yeah." He stroked her shoulder with gentle fingers sending goose bumps over her flesh.

"There was one photo I think Jess recognized. She acted funny after she saw it."

"Man? Woman?"

"A man. His clothes looked old. Like from the late 70's or early 80's."

"Hmm. She didn't say anything?"

"I asked her if she thought she knew him. She said she wasn't sure."

"That is strange." He turned over on his side to get face to face with her. "I thought I might have to kick Hayes's ass today."

Lori frowned. "What'd he do?" She was kind of irritated with Clint too. He was turning out to be one big jerk.

"He took off on me and Cook. Said he had some things to follow up on."

"He followed me and Jess, didn't he?" Lori knew it. What was he trying to prove?

Chet nodded. "I was pissed."

Lori shook her head. "I don't understand what he's doing. I always thought he was such a nice guy. That we were friends."

"You sure you weren't more than friends?"

Lori held back for a second, but she was wrong to do so. She wasn't keeping any secrets from this man. "Definitely just friends. My sister got into some trouble right before she graduated from high school. She and some other kids were at a party and there were drugs. A rap like that on her record would have knocked her out of the running for a scholarship she needed." She hoped Chet wouldn't hold this against her. "She was the only one at the party who was eighteen already. If no one else claimed the drugs, she was going down. I talked to Clint to get his legal advice since he has a law degree and he took care of it for me."

Chet studied her a moment. "Took care of it how?"

Lori chewed her lower lip and considered how to explain. "He called a friend of his and the charges were dropped. I don't know how. I didn't ask. He just did it. But," she went on, "I am relatively certain the method wasn't legal. I think the drugs went missing. It was all very hush-hush after that."

"Holy shit. I knew that guy was a sneaky SOB."

Lori nodded. "I guess so, but he sure did my sister a favor." She looked to Chet for understanding. "I owe him."

"Is that why you recommended him for the team?"

"I knew he wanted to move and he's a good cop."

Chet grunted. "Maybe."

"Does that make you think less of me?"

"No. You did what anyone would've done. If there was wrongdoing, it was on his part. You just let me know if he ever tries to get anything in return beyond the recommendation you gave."

"Don't worry," she warned, "if he tries getting anything else you won't have to kick his ass. I will."

# CHAPTER NINETEEN

Almost midnight. She couldn't believe she was really here. She damn sure couldn't believe *he* was here. His man had blindfolded her, tied her up, and then placed her in the trunk of the car. During the ride, she had dreamed of this moment. She didn't know how long it was before the car finally stopped and the trunk opened. Once she was untied and the blindfold removed, she'd been brought from the garage into the house. Not a house, she decided, a mansion.

Amanda Brownfield stared at the man she had idolized for so very long. She wanted him like nothing or no one she had ever wanted before. The pictures hadn't done him justice. He was so damned hot! She couldn't believe he wanted to meet her in person. To have her in his home. Her whole body burned with anticipation.

When he only stared back at her without saying a word, she moistened her lips and inclined her head so that her hair fell across her bare shoulder. She'd picked this strapless dress just for him. "I did everything like you asked."

"Your hair." He scrutinized her more closely with those piercing blues eyes.

She dared to move a little closer. A thrill shivered through her, made her wet. She wanted him to touch her. "I made it lighter just like you wanted."

"It's not right."

Her hopes of pleasing him deflated. By God, she'd bleached her hair as light as she could without frying the ends. It was almost right. Her lips puckered in petulance. Was he no different from every other man? Looking for something wrong with her. "What's wrong with my hair?"

He tangled his fingers in the long strands and pulled her even closer. "Hers is lighter."

She bit back a whimper of need as he twisted her hair more tightly around his fingers. If he didn't stop she was going to come standing right here. "I can fix it," she muttered breathlessly. She would do anything he asked… anything at all. She had been wrong to think he was like other men. There was no one else like him.

"Too late."

He yanked her head back. She gasped.

"You failed me," he whispered against her throat.

She leaned her body into his. "Then I guess you'll have to punish me."

He licked the pulse as the base of her throat. "Are you quite certain about that?"

She reached between their bodies and squeezed the bulge in his pants. "Yes." Her breath came in shallow puffs now. "I'm more than ready."

"You'll suffer pain as you have never suffered before."

She shivered. "Show me."

He led her into the front hall of his big ass mansion and then to the kitchen. He moved a cabinet with the press of a button. A hidden staircase appeared before them.

Her heart started to race in anticipation. "That's cool as hell. You got any other tricks to show me."

"You'll see." He gestured for her to go ahead of him. She moved down the stairs, her thighs quivering with building excitement. Finally, she was going to have him. She didn't care how much it hurt. She wanted Eric Spears deep inside her.

At the bottom of the stairs, she waited until the lights came on. Her eyes widened in amazement. The basement was gigantic. Everything was stainless steel, tile, and glass. The drains in the tile floor reminded her of the morgue when she'd gone with her mother to see her daddy's body. Stainless steel tables and tall glass boxes big enough to hold a person were arranged in the space. Just two tables but there were six of those strange boxes that looked kind of like shower enclosures. The kind that cost a lot of money. Two of the glass boxes were pitch black as if the intense fluorescent lights overhead couldn't penetrate to the interior.

She walked over to the sleek black glass and touched it. The darkness vanished and inside the box was a woman. She was asleep or dead. And naked. Her body was covered with the evidence of *his* attention. Amanda's nipples hardened just looking at the bruises and the cuts. The woman's chest rose with a shuddering breath. Not dead. The idea of sharing his attention tonight made Amanda a little jealous.

Moving to the next box, she touched it. The light came on and another woman was curled in the fetal position. She was naked too. Eric had played with her as well.

Neither was as pretty as Amanda. She was ready for her turn. The lights in the two boxes faded like a computer's screen saver, making the space beyond the glass go black again.

"Nice." She liked that the two in their glass cages had dark hair. He hadn't asked either of them to lighten their hair. That was probably because they were going to die. They weren't special like Amanda. He had told her that he had special plans for her.

"Take off the dress."

She reached behind her and lowered the zipper. Taking her time, she let the thin fabric slide down her body then she kicked it aside. She hadn't worn panties or a bra. Actually, she hadn't worn a bra since she was sixteen. She hated the damned things. No need. Her tits were awesome. High and firm. Even having a kid hadn't made 'em sag. Men always liked her tits.

Eric took a long look at her body before walking over to one of his shiny tables. "Lie down here."

She was so aroused she felt dizzy as she climbed onto the table and laid back. The steel was cold beneath her hot skin. Wouldn't take her long to warm it up, she was on fire. She purposely parted her thighs so he could see all she had to offer.

He strapped her to the table with her hands above her head and her legs spread a little wider. Then he rolled a smaller table next to her. He picked up something shiny from the tray of tools there.

"Do you know what this is?" He held it out for her to see.

"A scalpel."

He nodded as he moved closer and peered down at her.

She could hardly breathe she wanted him so bad. He teased her with the instrument, sliding it down her torso.

"This is going to be very painful," he promised.

She closed her eyes and waited for the sweet agony. "I'm ready."

The first burn of the blade made her come. She screamed with the delicious agony of it.

Then she begged for more.

# CHAPTER TWENTY

*Forty-one sets of remains.* Only six weren't human. It wasn't a record but it was right up there in the top ten. They were still assessing cause of death for most.

The road that accessed the farm had been closed on both sides of the property. Between the deputies and the Bureau, a decent perimeter had been made around the primary crime scene—the clearing around the house. The entire twenty acres was considered a secondary scene. There could be bodies anywhere in the woods and pastures.

"I've never seen anything like this," Corlew muttered.

Since Jess hadn't been able to talk to him last night, he'd come to Scottsboro this morning. Until now, they hadn't had a moment to themselves.

Sylvia was assisting the Jackson County coroner. The Bureau had put in a request for a forensic anthropologist to help with the identifications. Wallets had been buried with most of the remains, but not all. Identifying those victims would be far more complicated and well beyond Jess's pay grade. Even the remains with IDs would need confirmation. Closing this case would be a massive undertaking. It would take weeks if not months.

"Some go back decades." The ominous feeling that had been simmering deep inside her was edging closer to the surface. "We have victims whose driver's license expired in the 90s and since, but plenty more are from the 80s and earlier."

"You think it was the old woman. The victim found in the house?"

"Margaret?" Jess shrugged. "Maybe. Or maybe it was her father. According to a family friend, Margaret's father went to great lengths to keep men away from his daughter. I suppose Amanda's father could have been involved. He may even be one of the victims."

"You think the more recent ones are victims of Amanda."

"Possibly. Until we find her or some evidence that connects her to the murders, we can't say. There were traces of skin under the boyfriend's nails and we found cigarette butts we believe the killer left behind. Once we have her DNA for comparison, we can make that call."

"Why not use the kid's DNA?"

"That may turn out to be our only choice." Jess wanted to keep that little girl as far away from all this as possible. At some point, if they didn't find Amanda, Jess's hands would be tied and Maddie's

DNA would need to be used. It wasn't such a big deal. A quick mouth swab, but it just felt wrong.

Corlew scanned the goings-on around them. "Is this what you wanted to talk about? I tried to call you last night. When I saw the news I figured last night was not a good time."

"Let's sit in your car." She didn't want anyone to see or hear what she was about to do. She was breaking more than one law. She'd pushed a few boundaries in the past, but she'd never crossed the line. This was something she'd had to do.

She settled into the passenger seat of Corlew's car and waited for him to get behind the wheel. The windows were illegally tinted so she wasn't worried about anyone seeing what she was about to do.

Reaching into her bag, she removed the photo she'd taken from the house and passed it to Corlew. "That's my father."

He studied the guy in the photo. "Yeah. I've seen photos of him before." He turned to Jess. "What's the big deal about this one?"

"I found it here. In the house."

His gaze narrowed. "You found this" he held up the bag "here?"

She nodded.

He hissed a few choice words. "You know what you're doing, Jess?"

She nodded again.

He shrugged. "Okay, so these people somehow knew your father."

"I found the photo in a metal box hidden under the floorboards. Most of the other photos match the victims we've identified so far from their DMV photos."

Corlew took a second to digest the information before speaking. "He's not one of those unidentified victims out there, Jess. He and your mother died in that car crash. That I can confirm."

"A car crash that happened here…" Jess struggled to get air into her lungs. "In this county. Why is that, Buddy? Until I found that photo, I thought maybe it was a coincidence. They were visiting a friend or on a drive to nowhere in particular. But now I know better."

"We might never figure out why your parents were on that road in this county, but we know they were and we know that's where they died."

Jess snatched the photo back from him. "Then how did this get into that metal box in this house?"

"You showed me that wall. She's been watching you. Hell, Spears is digging up everything he can find on you. He may have found the photo and had it sent to this Amanda woman."

"The photo is old," Jess argued.

"Photos can be made to look old. You know that," Corlew argued. "Hell, the right geek can do anything with Photoshop. And didn't you tell me Spears visited Wanda and she showed him family photos? Maybe he took one of those when she wasn't looking?"

"What about that tree?" Jess tapped the photo again. "I believe this was taken right here in this yard."

"You think this is the only farm in north Alabama with an oak tree on it? It could've been taken anywhere."

So maybe she was overreacting. Spears could have taken one of her aunt's photos. Maybe. "I'm just not ready to put this on Spears. If he wanted me to see this photo, why not put it on the wall with all the others? This was hidden."

"He knows you, kid." Corlew lifted her chin and made her look at him. "He knew you'd keep looking for some clue as to who and what these people are. He likes the game. This is part of the fun for him. That's why you got the spray painted message on the car and the photo in the box. He's taunting you."

Corlew was right about that. "I think we have a family of murderers here. It's rare but not unheard of. Amanda may be one of Spears's groupies. He may have used her the way he did Richard Ellis and the Man in the Moon. But this…" Jess stared at the photo. "He's getting to me, Buddy." She met her old friend's gaze. "I can't trust myself to make the right decisions anymore."

He squeezed her hand. "The first thing you're going to do is turn that photo over as evidence. Then, you and your team will figure out this case, the same way you have all the others. You're too good to end up a screw-up like me, kid. Take my advice. Don't go down that path."

Jess leaned across the console and hugged him. Mostly to cover the tears she was struggling not to shed.

He patted her on the back. "You know this is going to start some serious rumors. I saw Gina Coleman strutting around out there."

Jess drew back, swiped away the damned tears. "She's my friend. She's trying to help figure out what's going on with Dan, too."

"Speaking of which, how's Danny boy taking the news about her sexual preference?"

Jess rolled her eyes. "Don't be a shit, Corlew."

He held his hands up. "So shoot me. It's a guy question." He shrugged. "She's still hot. Even if she is a lesbian."

The man was incorrigible. "Tell me what you've found—if anything. Did your arrest sever your connection with your source inside the BPD?"

"We had to cool it for a bit but we're good to go."

"You never said who your source is."

Buddy shook his head. "You don't need to know, Jess. Leave it at that."

She heaved a big sigh. "When I was working on the Five case, you alleged there were things in Dan's past I didn't know about. That he'd done some things in his capacity as chief that were wrong." It hurt to even say those words out loud. Corlew had to be mistaken about Dan. He would never do anything to harm anyone who didn't deserve it.

"You sure you want to hear this?"

Jess felt sick. "Yes."

"There were three cases while I was still a detective that I am certain Dan was somehow involved in the fix."

Jess shook her head. "That's impossible."

"Truth is," Corlew laughed, "I want to believe that too."

"Of course you do." He'd made her angry now. "If this is about your high school rivalry, I'm never speaking to you again, Corlew." How could she have hugged him just a few minutes ago?

"I'm serious, Jessie Lee."

She searched his face for any indication he was yanking her chain and found none. So maybe he was serious. "Explain."

He braced his hands on the steering wheel. Back in high school he'd driven a Harley. He'd been the coolest guy on either side of the tracks. Jess couldn't deny having been a little infatuated with him... until she met Dan. Now Corlew was a hotshot PI. She was counting on him to help her prove Dan was innocent.

"I've been crossing lines my whole life, Jess. I've even done a few things I won't admit to you or anyone else. Hell, it was the only way to survive. You know how it was growing up where we grew up."

She did, but she didn't say anything. She let him talk.

"A guy like me does what he has to do by hook or crook. Whatever it takes. I bust heads, carryout a little blackmail, tell a few lies, and hate the goody-two-shoes guys who are so clean they squeak when they walk. All that said, even I understand there has to be a few real heroes in this screwed up world. The kind of guy who stands for right and who never crosses too far over any line. The kind that bears the burden of guys like me." He heaved a big sigh. "No matter how much I've disliked Dan, I'd always seen him as one of the good guys until a few years ago. When I was kicked off the force, the idea that he was one of the bad guys was a big letdown. If Danny boy could be one of the bad guys, then no one could be trusted."

Jess sensed the truth in his words. This was the first time she'd ever seen this side of Corlew—the vulnerable guy under that macho façade.

"Now, I have reason to believe that Dan had nothing to do with what happened back then. I think it was a set up. You know, the kind those in power put in place to hedge their bets in case they need to keep you in line in the future."

"You think Pratt arranged for Dan's hands to look dirty just in case he ever had to get him under control."

Corlew nodded. "They groomed Dan for this position for years. Helped make him the most popular chief of police Birmingham has ever seen. The people love him. Their love and respect for Dan makes him powerful. Pratt and his pals knew that would be the case so they built in a safety net. Only they didn't count on one thing."

Jess smiled. "They underestimated his sense of integrity."

"Yep." Corlew laughed. "They didn't count on Danny boy being the real deal. He won't sacrifice his principles for anything except maybe you."

*And their child.*

"Can you prove he's innocent?"

Corlew sent her a sideways look. "Have you forgotten who you're talking to, kid? I will bust heads and squeeze every source I've got until I get what I need to do exactly that. Enough said."

Jess's hand trembled this time as she squeezed his arm. "Thank you." A rap on her window made her jump. She tucked the photo back into her bag as Corlew powered down the window.

Lori grimaced. "Sorry to interrupt."

Corlew wagged his eyebrows at her. "Detective, you can interrupt me any time day or night."

Jess shot him a look. "Thanks for stopping by, Corlew."

He held up his hands. "I know when I'm not wanted."

Jess got out of his car and watched her friend go. She hoped like hell he could pull this off. Dan's face had been all over the news this morning. Dority's testimony was damning. If Corlew could prove someone in the department was setting Dan up in the Allen case, maybe the same could be established about Dority's allegations.

"They're organizing the remains for removal," Lori explained. "I thought you'd want to oversee those efforts."

"Thanks." Jess retrieved the photo and handed it to Lori. "This needs to be logged into evidence."

Lori accepted the evidence bag. "This is the photo from the metal box?"

Jess took a deep breath. "Yes. The man's name is Lee Harris. He was my father."

Lori nodded. "Okay." She hesitated. "You sure about this?"

"As sure as I'll ever be." Jess gasped as she reached for Lori's left hand to have a look at her ring finger. "What's this?" How had she missed this glittering rock?

Lori grinned. "Chet proposed last night."

"That's great." Jess squeezed her hand before letting go. "Really great." How ironic that just a few weeks ago both she and Lori would have insisted that marriage was not even a bleep on their radars. "I guess Dan wasn't the only one with nuptials on his mind last night."

"The chief proposed?" Lori feigned surprise. "Did you say yes?"

"Like you're shocked." Jess shook her head. "He suggested we elope and I insisted we not do anything hasty. I did say I'd think about it though."

Lori shook her head adamantly from side to side. "No way. I need someone to commiserate with when the wedding planning starts. Isn't Dan's family Catholic?"

Jess waved her hands back and forth as if she could erase the subject. "No more talk about weddings." What she needed was something to calm her churning stomach. A Coke or even a Pepsi would do at this point. "Where's Lieutenant Hayes?"

"He's… ah… working with Dr. Baron." Lori cleared her throat and focused her attention on the evidence bag.

What was that all about? "Is something up with Hayes?"

"He wasn't interviewing neighbors yesterday, he was following us," she blurted, the hurt that went with that confession visible in her eyes. "I wasn't going to say anything but the more I think about it, the angrier I get. You told him to stay here and work with Harper and Cook, but he blew them off and followed us." Lori looked away as she lost control of her emotions. "He was concerned that I wouldn't be able to protect you if the need arose." She shrugged. "Maybe he's right and that's what I'm mad about."

Jess barely restrained a rush of outrage. "Take care of that evidence. I'll speak to Hayes."

As she marched around the open graves, Jess was glad she'd made this another blue jeans and sneakers day. Though the ground was dry, there was still a lot of digging and climbing about in the dirt to be done. There was no reason they shouldn't all be comfortable. The only suits lurking around were the two agents, one of whom was Todd Manning from the Birmingham Field Office.

Then there was Clint Hayes who stood out like a model from a more mature Abercrombie ad. He might look like the perfect guy on the outside with his expensive clothes and his handsome face, but as detectives went he had a lot to learn. His ego kept getting in the way of his good sense.

"Lieutenant, I need a moment," she announced as she came alongside him.

Hayes gave her a nod and then followed her to the barn. So far, no unmarked graves in there, which assured it would be empty. When they were deep enough inside the gloomy structure to avoid being seen or heard, she turned on him.

"We need to get a few things straight."

He crossed his arms over his chest. "You have my undivided attention, Chief."

"As I told you yesterday, SPU is a team." She took a moment to get her temper under control. "On this team, there is only one rank that matters and that's mine. Everyone else is equal regardless of pay grade. But," she warned, "if I'm forced to select my second in command it will be Sergeant Harper, not you. I would suggest you not push me to make that choice since you're still on probation. I am inordinately unhappy to discover that you not only disobeyed orders yesterday, you lied to me. You weren't interviewing neighbors, you were following me."

"I did what I had to do to ensure you stayed safe," he argued with absolutely no repentance. "Harper told you, didn't he?" Before Jess could answer, Hayes held up his hands. "No, wait. It was Wells. She shared their pillow talk with you and now I'm busted."

The man just didn't know when to shut up. "Do you think I'm blind, Lieutenant?" There was no holding back her ire now. "Or perhaps you think I'm not as smart as you are because I'm a woman and I don't have a law degree."

"You're putting words in my mouth, Chief. I'd be a fool not to recognize your intelligence level as well as the caliber of cop you are."

"Then there must be something else making you act like a fool, Lieutenant, because that's exactly how you're behaving. Foolhardy. That will not keep you on this team. There's no place for grandstanding on my team."

"You're overreacting. I followed my instincts. I took a risk. Don't tell me you've never taken one. Or opted not to trust someone you should have."

Did the man have no concept of when he should shut up? "Are you under the mistaken assumption the secret you figured out somehow gives you an advantage over the others?"

"Again," he pointed out in that arrogant manner only those trained to be an attorney could pull off, "you're putting words in my mouth."

He wasn't taking this or her seriously. "You're done for the day, Lieutenant."

"Hold on a minute, Chief."

"You hold on a minute," she cautioned. "At this particular minute I am madder than hell. I'm trying to give you the opportunity to let me cool off before I write you up for disobeying orders and insubordination." She squared her shoulders and lifted her chin. "We'll talk when I'm back at the office. Now, go, Lieutenant, before I show you what it looks like when I really do overreact."

As her newest detective walked away, Jess did some slow, deep breathing in an effort to calm down.

Everything was unraveling way too fast. For the first time in her life, she was almost afraid to even think what would happen next.

"Don't borrow trouble, Jess."

# CHAPTER TWENTY ONE

Dan stood at the window overlooking the city he loved. He should call Jess and warn her about the latest charge against him. He hated like hell to give her anything else to worry about. She had more than enough on her plate already. This one would really get to her. She would probably be required to give a statement.

Lieutenant Valerie Prescott had filed an EEO complaint against him related to her transfer from SPU. In retrospect, Dan fully understood he hadn't handled her reassignment as diplomatically as he would have had he not been operating on emotion. Jess had warned him there could be trouble over his rash decision.

What was done, was done.

He'd tried to contact Meredith twice but she hadn't returned his calls. His attorney had warned him not to do that either, but Dan hadn't listened. He couldn't fathom why she would do this. Prescott he understood. The woman was pissed at being passed over for the position he offered to Jess, and Prescott wanted to get even. There was nothing like that in his history with Meredith. What did she possibly hope to gain?

Dan shoved his hands into his pockets. After the breakup with Jess more than two decades ago, he'd been back in Birmingham barely a year when he and Meredith married. He closed his eyes. God, he had missed Jess so damned bad. Every part of him had been aching. He'd needed someone to fill that void. Meredith had been right there in front of him. Two years older, she'd been such a good friend. Things had escalated from there. No more than a year after their hasty marriage, she had known what he should have known all along, he was still in love with Jess.

He and Meredith had parted on good terms. For several years more, they had continued to work together. She'd moved to Montgomery and the governor's staff about the same time he became chief of police. He'd run into her from time to time since but not recently. Not until this week.

Pratt had to be behind her decision to launch this abrupt smear campaign. The question was what did Pratt have on Meredith? Dan couldn't believe she would do this without pressure from someone.

A knock at his door dragged him back from the troubling thoughts. "Come on in." He fully expected it to be Black with even more bad news.

Clint Hayes walked in and closed the door behind him.

Another line of apprehension joined the others furrowing Dan's brow. "Is Chief Harris back in her office?"

Hayes shook his head. "She dismissed me for the day." He shrugged. "I have a feeling I'm barely hanging on by a thread with her and the team."

Dan exhaled a frustrated breath. "I warned you not to give her any trouble. That chip you carry around isn't conducive to making friends, Lieutenant." What the hell? He needed this guy keeping an eye on Jess.

"You told me to watch her, but the others didn't want me horning in too close to the boss. I can safely say that, this time, my attitude had little or nothing to do with my current dilemma."

Dan had his doubts about that. "What're you going to do about this, Lieutenant?"

Hayes turned his hands up. "I'm open to suggestions on how to get back in her good graces."

Dan wasn't fixing this for him. "I'm confident you'll figure it out if you want to remain a part of the SPU."

Hayes nodded in acknowledgment. "You're the boss." He started to go but then hesitated and faced Dan once more. "Buddy Corlew paid a visit to the crime scene today. He and Chief Harris had a lengthy private meeting. It seems you're not the only one keeping secrets."

For about two seconds, Dan weighed the ramifications of punching the lieutenant in the face. Why give Pratt more ammunition? "I suggest you follow the order Chief Harris gave you, Lieutenant. We have nothing further to discuss."

When the door closed, Dan kicked his chair. It banged off the credenza but he didn't care. If he thought for one second Hayes had intended the comment as informative he might not have wanted to punch him.

What the hell was Corlew meeting privately with Jess about? Was he going to join the cause and go to the press with his own theories of how Dan had handled cases in the past? He'd already tried to make Dan and the department look bad on several occasions. What was one more? Or maybe he'd file a complaint against Dan too. After all, he was the one to fire Corlew.

If he was filling Jess's head with his delusions, Dan would...

He laughed. "What're you going to do, Burnett? Kick the guy's ass?"

He plowed a hand through his hair. How did he fight this? Prescott's complaint would amount to nothing more than her word against his—a nuisance, at best. If Corlew had ever had any real evidence against Dan or the department, for that matter, he would have brought it forward long ago. Pratt was annoyed that he wasn't getting his way.

Meredith and Allen were the two unknown variables. His attorney had his work cut out for him because Dan sure as hell had no idea where this was coming from.

Unless it was Spears.

If it was, how was he supposed to fight a ghost?

Dan checked his cell. Somehow he kept hoping he'd hear from the son of a bitch. Now that Spears had him where he wanted him there was no need for Spears to bother, Dan supposed. Spears was a coward. He wasn't man enough to do this himself.

As if to refute his assertion, he felt a twinge in his side. Dan gritted his teeth. Even when the bastard stabbed him, he'd waited until Dan was restrained.

Another knock drew his attention to the door. He'd sent Sheila home early. He'd gotten a heads up about Prescott's announcement in time to see that his secretary as well as his receptionist were out of the building before the press gathered outside for a statement.

Harold Black stuck his head in. "You have a few minutes, Dan?"

Dan had a feeling things were about to get worse. "Of course." He motioned to the chairs in front of his desk. "Make yourself at home."

Four years ago when Dan was selected for this position, Harold had been greatly disappointed. His unhappiness had been public knowledge in the department. The tension had lasted a few weeks. Ultimately, Dan had invited him to knock back a few beers and they'd talked it through. From that moment, he and Harold had worked closely together. Never any trouble. They'd gone back to being the kind of friends they had always been.

Until Jess came home.

Dan suddenly understood how hard it must be for her to deal with all this. She felt as if it was her fault.

It wasn't her fault.

Harold passed a file to Dan before taking his seat. "That's the Fire Marshal's report on the fire at your home. He's officially calling it arson. The fire started in the kitchen. The accelerant was charcoal starter."

Dan tossed the report aside. He didn't need to see it. He'd known it was arson. What he hadn't known was the source. "The same stuff I keep in my garage for the occasional family barbecue, am I right?"

Harold nodded solemnly.

"You know this is so damned contrived that it's laughable." Dan shook his head. "Why would I set my house on fire—to destroy evidence—" he pointed out "with an accelerant I keep in my garage?"

Harold sighed. "I said the same thing to the Mayor just before I came over here."

Dan did laugh this time. "I'll bet he's eating this up."

"He's not happy."

As if Dan gave a damn. "He can go to hell, Harold. You can tell him I said so." The man was trying to take Dan down and he wasn't going to go down without a fight. "There are things I could be taking to the press about Pratt, but that's not the way I operate. He's counting on that."

"Dan." Harold held up his hands in a stop sign gesture. "It's not going to do anybody any good to start this kind of back and forth with the mayor. What we need is containment. We need to shut this down not fuel it."

Fury whipped inside him. "You're telling me this?" He leaned forward and slapped his palms against his desk. "Who do you think kept Joe Pratt out of trouble all those years?"

"You don't have to convince me, Dan." He shook his head. "I'm grasping at straws trying to find reason in the unreasonable."

Dan's rage withered. There was more. "I appreciate you delivering the Fire Marshal's report, but clearly you have something else on your mind."

"Internal Affairs is asking questions. This was not a good situation in the first place, Dan, and it just got worse. Pratt is pushing hard for action. The Dority and Prescott business lends credence to the stand he's taken against you."

"So this is it." Dan got it now. "He wants me gone that bad."

"If you choose not to take a leave of absence, as I suggested, you will eventually be placed on administrative leave. You know how this works, Dan. You can't run this office during an investigation of this magnitude."

Jess needed him to be smart about this. Their child needed the same. Whatever he did at this critical juncture could come back to haunt them all. He didn't want his child to come into this world with him in prison.

Dear God. There was no stopping this.

So be it. If he was going down, he might as well be here for Jess as long as possible. If he were out of the loop, he would be blind to what was going on with Spears. He couldn't take that risk. Jess needed him here, doing all he could to keep her safe. Their child needed him.

"You tell Pratt I'll be in this office until they escort me out." With that out of the way, Dan stood. "I think we've both said all there is to say."

Harold pushed to his feet. "Dan, please, take the evening and think about this. Talk it over with Jess. Every move you make is going to be weighed in this investigation. Don't give them anything else to use against you."

Dan smiled for his old friend. "I appreciate your advice, but my mind is made up."

"Moving forward," Harold said soberly, "I won't be able to discuss the case with you. I hope you understand."

That was the one thing Dan could say without reservation. He completely understood. "I understand completely."

The door closed behind Harold, the sound echoing in the silence.

Dan exhaled a heavy breath. He was going home. He could stop by the market and pick up something nice for dinner and flowers for Jess. She would be exhausted when she came home. Maybe a nice dinner followed by a hot bath and a long, slow massage to help her relax.

He locked up and headed out of the building. Better to get an estimated time she would be home before preparing dinner. He tapped her name in his contact list and waited through the four rings.

Outside, the heat and humidity hanging in the air had him loosening his tie. When the greeting for her voicemail was finished, he left her a message. "I know you're busy. Let me know when you're heading home. I'll have dinner waiting." He checked the street before crossing. "I love you, Jess. Be careful out there."

He tucked the phone into his jacket pocket and removed his keys. The brisk walk to the parking garage cleared his head a bit. Or maybe it was just hearing Jess's recorded voice when he'd called. Keeping perspective was particularly important right now. There was no room for emotions in this situation. He was down a few points, but the match wasn't over yet.

As he entered the level where his parking space was reserved, he hit the clicker and started the engine so the interior of his SUV would start to cool. His mother had called today to apologize again for her behavior last night. Dan was grateful she was making the effort. He hoped one day she and Jess could be friends in the truest sense of the word.

A laugh rumbled in his chest. "Miracles happen." He hit the unlock button as he reached his SUV and climbed in. He fastened his seat belt and backed out of the parking slot. Somehow focusing on the mundane felt comfortable. As he exited the garage, a strange odor had him frowning. Maneuvering into going home traffic, he sniffed a couple of times. What the hell was that smell? Coppery. Metallic…

*Blood.*

Before his foot reached the brake, something cold and hard jammed into the back of his skull.

*Gun.*

"Keep driving."

He glanced at the rearview mirror. Didn't immediately recognize the female face staring back at him. Then he knew…

*Amanda Brownfield.*

"Hello, Chief Burnett." She grinned. "It's nice to finally meet you."

"What do you want?" He dropped his left hand into his lap. His cell phone was in his pocket.

"Both hands on the wheel, Chief," she warned with a nudge of the barrel of her weapon.

He lifted his hand back to the wheel. "Are you injured?" The smell of blood was even stronger now.

"I'll do the talking and you do the listening."

He met her gaze in the rearview mirror. "All right."

"We're going home to wait for Jess. You take me there without any trouble and you might just live through this night, Chief."

Dan focused his attention on driving but his mind was reeling off scenarios to stop this woman's plan.

"Good boy," she said. "You just keep driving and we won't have any trouble."

Dan settled on a course of action. "Whatever you say."

# CHAPTER TWENTY TWO

Jess walked the length of the case board. Copies of the photos from the metal box now formed a time-line. Harper and Lori were working to match the names of victims with dates of disappearance.

So far, they had forty-one sets of remains. Although wallets and other personal effects had been buried with some, those identities would need to be confirmed.

"Ben Parks," Harper said, "reported missing July, five years ago."

Lori added the date beneath his photo.

Some of the remains were far older than five years. Jess studied the many faces staring out at her. How long had Amanda and, possibly, her mother and/or grandfather been taking lives? The part that didn't make sense was the money. Most of the wallets they'd found still contained money. If the

Brownfields weren't killing for the money, what was the motive?

Was the father, Lawrence, involved? How far back in the family tree did the killing go? What about Amanda's grandmother? She had died before Amanda was born, but had she been a killer too?

"If," Jess said aloud, "Margaret and Amanda were both a part of the murders, why was Margaret murdered?" She turned to Lori. "The boyfriend's idea? A family quarrel? Or maybe Margaret found God and decided the killing had to stop?"

"According to the boyfriend's mother," Lori reminded her, "Margaret rarely attended church."

"She did say that, didn't she?" Jess tapped a dry erase marker against her chin. "Maybe Margaret started to make mistakes as she grew older and Amanda decided it was time for her to retire? Something may have happened to prevent her from burying her mother before her body was found. Leaving the body was a deviation from her previous MO."

"Except," Hayes said as he strolled up to the case board, "we know she was busy dropping off her daughter for Eric Spears. Maybe she was too focused on pleasing him to be concerned with her dead mother."

"A reasonable theory." Jess slanted him a glance. She was still annoyed with the lieutenant. "Why the sudden decision not to keep the family secret anymore?" Jess looked from one detective to the next. Everyone was present except Cook. He'd stayed at the crime scene along with two Jackson County deputies who had dubbed the place the Body Farm. The three would be staying the night. "Then again, according to the boyfriend's mother, Margaret despised what her daughter did to animals. It stands to reason she wouldn't be pleased with Amanda murdering a person either."

Lori opened her mouth to offer an answer but Hayes beat her to the draw. "Whatever role her mother played, Amanda doesn't need the family anymore." He tapped her photo. "She has Spears now. He's her ticket to get out of that one-horse town. It's a story as old as time."

If he was trying to impress Jess, he was making headway. She passed him the marker. "Now that's good, Lieutenant."

A smile quirked one corner of his mouth. "Thank you, Chief."

He made the notes under Amanda's photo. Harper called out more names and dates. Lori updated the status of each victim's photo.

Maybe the deputies were right. This was a body farm. Whatever it was, they needed to find Amanda Brownfield. She was the key to this bizarre case.

Jess grabbed another marker and started a list of potential motives. Power. Lust. Cannibalism. Organ harvesting.

She hesitated. "Lieutenant, see if Amanda or her mother were active on eBay or any other international trade outlet. We can't rule out the possibility that they were selling organs for any number of purposes. Check to see if anyone in the family had any medical training." Jess pursed her lips in thought before adding, "While you're at it, find out if Margaret, her husband or someone else who lived on the farm ever operated a restaurant or food service business of any sort."

"Oh," Lori made a face, "that's just sick."

Jess shrugged. "They were supporting themselves somehow." Inside, where the others couldn't see, she shuddered at the idea as well. "On the other hand, since all the buried victims are male, maybe this is a purge. Amanda's father left her, according to Mrs. Clements. Margaret's father was an overbearing disciplinarian. Maybe Amanda and her mother were doing their part to purge the earth of the male species."

Harper grunted. "That's harsh."

"Some of us only feel that way on occasion," Jess assured him.

A rap on the door preceded its opening. Harold Black stepped in and looked around. "Chief Harris, have you heard from Burnett?"

"We just returned from Jackson County. He left me a voicemail that he was going home for the day." She'd tried to call him back but there'd been no answer. "Can I help you with something?"

"Sergeant Harper, why don't you try and track Chief Burnett down," Black suggested. "Let him know we're in need of his presence. Chief Harris, you and I are wanted in the conference room. Agent Gant has an update on the Spears investigation. He's setting up a conference call as we speak."

Jess's stomach took a little tumble. "Detective Wells, give Harper a hand." She turned to Hayes. "Lieutenant, you may come with me."

Jess grabbed her bag and her phone and followed Black from her office. Every nerve in her body was on alert.

BPD CONFERENCE ROOM, 7:15 P.M.

Jess sat stiffly in the chair next to the empty one where Dan should be sitting. Gant droned on with his update. Dan still wasn't answering his phone. She'd heard nothing from Lori and Harper. Her instincts were screaming at her to walk out of this conference room and find Dan herself.

This was not like him.

Mayor Pratt, Agent Todd Manning from the local Bureau office, and Harold Black sat around the table asking all the usual questions to which Gant had absolutely no new answers. They had no idea where Spears was or what he was doing. There had been no new abductions. No developments on the two missing women, Rory Stinnett and Monica Atmore.

Why were they wasting time in this damned meeting?

"Excuse me," Jess interrupted. All eyes swung to her. "Agent Gant, I'm in the middle of a case with a killer or killers who have planted a whole crop of bodies. If you could, please cut to the chase. Do you have anything relevant I need to know? If not, I'll get out of the way so that you," she smiled at the glower-ing looks directed at her, "and these fine gentlemen may carry on."

Gant stared out at her from the monitor deliver-ing his image all the way from Quantico. His frustra-tion couldn't have been clearer had she been sitting across the desk from him as she had many, many times when she was a profiler.

"We have narrowed down the one IP address we captured amid all the chatter about you on the Internet."

The last she'd heard the chatter had stopped, but they had been able to lock onto one IP address. The user was somewhere within a one-hundred-fifty mile radius of the city. The transmission had been bouncing between Atlanta, Nashville, and Birmingham. This was nothing new.

When she would have said as much, Gant con-tinued, "We now know those transmissions were sent from the Birmingham area. Within a twenty-five mile radius of your current location."

The cold circling around her suddenly started to sink deep into her bones.

"Are you confirming that Spears is here? In Birmingham still?" Black asked what everyone else in the room no doubt wanted to know.

"We believe so," Gant allowed. "That could change hour to hour or day to day, but we are con-vinced he's staying close. That's why we haven't been able to pick him up again. He's laying low. Waiting to strike."

Jess's phone vibrated. She jumped. She'd put it on silent for the meeting but she'd kept it in her hand in hopes of hearing from Dan.

Harper's name and image flashed on the screen.

"I have to take this," she muttered. She hurried away from the table. "Did you find him?"

"Yes, ma'am." A beat of silence passed. "The chief was in an accident. He's at the ER. I'm waiting for you in front of the building."

"How bad is he hurt?" Jess demanded, her heart in her throat.

Another of those long trauma-filled moments elapsed before Harper went on. "In addition to injuries related to crash, he suffered a gunshot wound to the head. His condition is unclear at this time. We should go *now*, ma'am."

"I'm on my way, Sergeant." Feeling numb, Jess ended the call and strode to her chair. She grabbed her bag. "I have to go to the hospital. Dan's been in an accident."

She ignored the barrage of questions fired at her as she hurried from the conference room.

Hayes called her name and rushed after her as she hurried down the corridor but she ignored him too. The way her body was shaking, if she slowed down she would fall.

She had to get to Dan.

# CHAPTER TWENTY THREE

Jess sat on the edge of the narrow hospital bed and cradled Dan's hand in hers. "You were lucky." Her throat was so dry, those three words croaked out of her. This was too close. Way too close.

"I knew what I was doing." He propped an arm behind his head, then winced with the pain of moving any part of his body. The bandage on the left side of his forehead covered the stitches where the bullet had grazed him.

The idea of how lucky he was to be alive made her head spin and her heart lurch. A few millimeters farther to the left and the bullet would have entered the frontal lobe rather than glancing off his forehead.

"You crashed your fancy car." Jess shook her head as she worked to keep the damned tears at bay. She'd already embarrassed herself on the way here by crying in front of Harper. "You aimed right

242

VILE

for that abandoned building." She exhaled a shaky breath. "You could've been killed."

"She would have killed me anyway," he reminded her. "You, too, if I'd taken her to the apartment to wait for you to come home."

"You almost killed my prime suspect." Jess swiped at her damp cheeks and sniffed. "It's a miracle she survived. How could I question her if she was dead?" Irritation shoved aside some of the weaker emotions. "How am I supposed to solve this case without her? All those victims deserve justice. What were you thinking?"

He grinned, then groaned. "That I wanted to protect you. That you and our child are more important to me than any case."

Jess would not cry again. She closed her eyes for a second. "Okay. I suppose I would've done the same thing." She shrugged. "Maybe."

He laughed and grabbed his stomach. He had two cracked ribs from the seatbelt. "I guess that's as close to a compliment as I'm going to get. And I thought I was being a hero."

Jess wanted to slug him. This was no laughing matter. She didn't need a hero. She needed him. "You might consider choosing a softer target next time. Like some shrubbery or a fence."

"I'd rather there not be a next time." He tugged her down for a kiss. "Keeping you and the baby safe was all I could think about." He caressed her cheek. "I love you, Jess. I'm not letting anyone take you from me."

She smiled, stretched to give him another kiss. "I love you. You needn't worry. I'm not going anywhere without you."

A tap on the door brought reality crashing in before Jess was ready. She wished they could just disappear for a while, but that wouldn't change anything. Spears would still be waiting to taunt her with another victim. He wouldn't stop until he was dead.

The door opened just far enough for Lori to slip into the room. "Chief Harris, you asked me to let you know when Amanda Brownfield was moved to a room. Sheriff Foster says you can question her now."

"Thanks. I'll be right there." Jess kissed Dan on the chin before easing off the bed. "I'll be back as soon as I'm finished. Maybe she'll give me some answers." Wishful thinking probably. If nothing else, they had Brownfield in custody now. She couldn't hurt anyone else—especially not her daughter.

Maddie was another part of this case that wouldn't have a particularly happy ending. The child might as well be an orphan. The people she was supposed to depend on had let her down.

"I'll be here," Dan promised.

Those words reminded Jess of the upside in this mess. Dan was alive. For that, she was immensely grateful. He sustained a mild concussion where his head bounced off the driver's side window. The doctor was keeping him overnight for observation. Jess didn't want him moving from this room until they were positive he was okay.

Feeling a little wobbly, she paused at the door to steady herself and to flash him a smile. "I'm counting on that."

Outside the room, her detectives waited with the two uniformed officers standing guard. "Sergeant, you and the lieutenant stay here." Jess turned to Lori. "Detective Wells, let's go see what Miss Brownfield has to say for herself."

Jess had a few things to say to her as well.

When Hayes would have objected, Jess shot him a look that she hoped reminded him of his place. Evidently, it did because he gave a nod and kept his mouth shut.

"I let Cook know what's going on," Lori said as they moved toward the bank of elevators. "He asked if you needed him back in Birmingham."

Jess shook her head. "He should stay at the scene in case there are any developments overnight. We'll be there first thing in the morning."

"I'll let him know."

While Lori sent Cook a text, Jess considered what she'd been told about Brownfield's condition. Like Dan, she had a concussion. Since she hadn't been wearing a seatbelt, she also had a fractured collarbone and dislocated shoulder from her flight over the console and an up close encounter with the dash. Lucky for her, the first point of impact had been her shoulder rather than her head.

Jess was so tired. Now that she'd seen firsthand that Dan was okay, she felt as weak as a kitten. Not a good place to be when interviewing a suspect, but it had to be done. Her cell chimed and she fished in her bag for the confounded thing. The elevator car arrived with a ding of warning. Her stomach growled a warning of its own about dinner. She really had to eat soon. The doors slid open and Jess boarded. She leaned against the wall and checked the screen of her cell. Lori stepped inside and tapped the proper button for Brownfield's floor.

Jess frowned and then the image on the screen stole her breath. Long flowing brown hair… dark eyes and a big smile. The photo of the young woman was followed by another text. *Isn't she lovely, Jess?*

"Oh my god." He'd taken another victim…

*See you soon.*

The elevator stopped but Jess couldn't move.

Lori looked from the phone to Jess. "Is it him?"

Jess nodded and handed her cell to Lori. "Victim number three." The game was progressing.

"Jesus Christ." Lori's face went pale. She passed the cell back to Jess. "We're never going to be able to stop him, are we?"

Determination hardened inside Jess. "Oh yes we are." She stormed out of the elevator. And she knew exactly where to start.

As she strode down the corridor, Jess mentally reviewed the rest of the report given to her earlier by the doctor who had examined Amanda Brownfield. Numerous, recent lacerations marred her torso and her thighs. Since the pelvic and thigh bruising suggested sexual assault, a rape kit had been taken.

VILE

Brownfield had been semiconscious and unable to answer questions when she arrived in the ER. Taking the rape kit under the circumstances was SOP. One look at the photos of her injuries and Jess knew who was responsible. She recognized the pattern of torture the Player used on his victims.

Only Amanda Brownfield wasn't dead.

Whatever she knew about Spears, Jess intended to learn before this day ended.

Two Jackson County deputies, Sheriff Foster, as well as a Birmingham officer were stationed outside Brownfield's room.

As Jess approached, Foster shook his head. "She won't talk to me beyond screaming profanities. She did ask for you between shouting matches. We've taken all precautions with wrist and ankle restraints as well as a waist shackle. She's not getting out of that bed until we let her out."

"Thank you, Sheriff." Jess turned to Lori. "She may not talk with you in the room."

Lori didn't look convinced. "You sure you want to do this alone?"

"Absolutely." Jess forwarded to Lori's cell the photo Spears had sent. "See that Chief Black and Agent Gant get that ASAP."

"Will do."

Jess gave her a nod and then reached for the door. She dismissed the idea that she was still wearing jeans and sneakers, both dirty from exploring graves all day. At least the t-shirt with its BPD logo looked official.

Amanda Brownfield watched Jess enter the room. She didn't speak, just watched. Jess placed her bag on the floor at the end of the bed before moving to the raised side rail. "Hello, Amanda. I'm—"

"I know who you are." Her voice was strong. A little raspy, probably from years of smoking. "Deputy Chief Jess Harris," she said mockingly.

"Of course." Jess smiled. "You've been keeping up with me."

"No law against that," Brownfield argued.

"No law against that," Jess agreed. "Would you like to know how your daughter's doing?"

"Doesn't matter. My momma ruined her, made her too needy and clingy." Brownfield tilted her head and eyed Jess. "You can have her."

Jess bit back the response that came immediately to mind. "Well then, why don't you tell me about the human remains we found on your farm?"

Brownfield considered Jess for a bit before answering. "What makes you think I know anything about those?"

"Forty-one sets of remains have been uncovered so far," Jess pressed on. "You must have some idea how that happened. After all, you've lived on that farm for most of your life."

Brownfield shrugged her left shoulder and grimaced. Her right arm was immobilized in a sling, which made securing her right hand problematic. Foster had fastened it to the waist shackle. The left was secured to the rail on the opposite side of the bed. "Maybe my grandparents built on a cemetery.

How am I supposed to know what they did before I was born?"

"Your family has owned the property for seventy years, but some of the remains we found are far more recent. For instance, Brock Clements, your boyfriend. We found his body, Amanda. I don't think your grandparents had anything to do with his murder."

Brownfield hummed a note of boredom. "Since you have it all figured out, what do you want me to say?"

This case was far from *all figured out.* It would likely be months before the numerous victims were officially identified, causes of death confirmed, and murderers and motives nailed down. "You could start with the truth," Jess recommended. The sheriff had already questioned Brownfield. She was well aware of her rights, and so far she hadn't asked for an attorney. If Jess were lucky, she wouldn't change her mind now.

Brownfield grinned, an expression that confirmed Jess's assessment of her—she felt no responsibility much less remorse for her actions. She was a pathological liar. Had frequent, short-term relationships and was manipulative and cunning, impulsive and callous. Her list of character flaws went on and on. Bottom line, Amanda Brownfield was a true psychopath.

"You sure you can handle the truth, Jess?" she taunted.

"Why don't you try me?"

"All right." Brownfield sighed, the sound one of satisfaction. She was enjoying this. "My granddaddy taught me how to spot the best targets. The ones who deserved to die the most. He showed me how good it felt to take a life. It's like a drug. Once you're addicted, you just can't stop. But," she qualified, "if you're smart, you make sure the target can't be traced back to you. I guess I screwed up on that one."

A chill swept through Jess. A multi-generational family of killers was rare, but the Brownfields were fitting squarely into that category. "How did you and your grandfather choose your targets?"

Brownfield shrugged. "It's not something you can put into words. It's a feeling. You just know who has to die."

Braced for the answer she didn't want to hear, Jess asked the question haunting her. "Why did you keep the pictures?"

"My granddaddy liked keeping a record. We used to make up stories about them. It passed the time." Brownfield smiled knowingly. "Did you find one you liked?"

Jess rummaged in her bag for her cell. She'd snapped a pic of the photo of her father. She showed it to Brownfield. "Tell me his story. The real one."

Amanda barely glanced at the screen. "*He's* waiting for you." She smiled. "You're all he talks about—you and this special game he has planned."

"Are you referring to the man in the photo?" Jess wasn't going to play games with this woman. She needed direct answers not more riddles.

"You know who I'm talking about."

"I need a name, Amanda." A flare of anger gave an edge to her demand.

"Eric." Brownfield said his name as if she was a teenager and he was her current celebrity crush. "The *Player*. He told me everything."

"Really?" Jess showed her the photo of Spears's latest victim—the one she'd received only minutes ago. "Did he tell you about her? Is she part of his special game too?"

Brownfield executed another of those listless shrugs. "I've never seen her before in my life."

"Then he didn't share everything with you, Amanda. He used you." Jess opted for a new tactic, putting her on the defensive. "And now he's finished with you. He doesn't need you anymore."

That knowing smile returned. "Maybe, but there are plenty of others waiting for a turn to serve him."

"Others?" Jess held her breath.

"People like me, who'll do anything he asks."

This following Spears had amassed was the part Jess couldn't fully comprehend. What was it about him that motivated so many to do his bidding? There was always a motive. Always. What was she missing?

"How did he find you?" Jess pressed on. "Where did you first meet?"

"I'm tired now." Brownfield looked away. "You should leave. Eric won't like it if I tell you too much."

Jess's heart pounded so hard she could barely hear herself think. This woman was alive. She had done Spears' bidding, come face to face with him, and survived. Whatever information she had, Jess wanted it. *Now*. "Why did he pick you?"

Brownfield turned back to Jess. "I thought you'd figured that out already." A slow smile slid across her face. "It's our connection."

"What connection?" The photo of the man who was almost certainly her father flashed in Jess's mind.

"The man in the photo you showed me," Brownfield said, seemingly hearing Jess's thought. "*Our* father. He died when I was six, but then you know that, don't you? My momma and I went to the coroner's office to see him. He was lying on that steel table with your momma on the one right next to him. My momma kissed him goodbye and then she made me do it. She loved him a lot, you know."

Images of her father and mother laid out on cold slabs flashed in Jess's mind. One endless moment passed before she could speak. "Your father's name was Lawrence Howard. The Cadillac in the barn was registered to him."

Brownfield shook her head. "That's just the name he used when he was with us. His real name was Lee Harris. I'm your sister, Jess. No use fighting it."

Jess restrained the fierce emotions clawing at her. "Is this another of the stories like the ones you and your grandfather made up?"

"Do a DNA test," Brownfield dared. "I know who I am. That's why Eric wanted inside me. He knows we have the same blood flowing through our veins. Having me was the next best thing to having you."

Jess refused to believe her outrageous story. It wasn't possible... and yet, she instinctively understood there was some aspect of truth in her words.

"When was the last time you were contacted by Eric Spears?" Just saying his name out loud made Jess want to vomit. Whatever this woman's story, finding and stopping Spears was all that mattered.

"Today."

Shock radiated through Jess. She already knew the answer to the question she was about to ask, but she couldn't stop the words from tumbling out. "Where did you meet with him?"

"I was blindfolded and put into a trunk by his man. I have no clue how we got to Eric's home, but it wasn't that far from here."

"What man?" Jess went on alert. "Do you know his name? Can you give me a description of him and the house?"

"The man wore a mask. I didn't see anything except the inside of the house."

"Start at the beginning and tell me everything Spears said to you and everything you saw inside his home." Jess felt ice cold. She gripped the bed's side rail to ensure she stayed vertical. He was here. *Close.*

"He gave me instructions and a key fob that worked on your honey's SUV. He provided the gun he wanted me to use. After that, he told me to take off my dress." Brownfield smiled. "He's the best lover I ever had and that, sister, is all I got to say."

"That's all he said to you?" Jess struggled for a deep breath. This woman had been with Spears... *here*. She had to know more than she was telling.

Brownfield heaved a big sigh. "Okay, okay. There was just one other thing you might want to know."

Jess held her breath.

"When he came," she licked her lips as if she could still taste him, "he screamed your name."

Jess wanted to shake her. To twist that damaged arm until she told anything else she knew. "That doesn't say much for you, does it, Amanda?"

Rage colored the other woman's cheeks. "Here's a newsflash, *Chief Harris*. Eric knows your secret."

Jess drew back. He couldn't possibly know...

Brownfield laughed long and loud. "I thought that might shake things up. He's coming for you, Jess. You're wasting your time fighting the inevitable."

Jess's cell made that little chime that notified her when she received a text message. Feeling disjointed, she swiped the screen to open it.

*Congratulations, Jess. It's a shame Dan won't live to see his child.*

Jess's heart dropped. *Spears knew.*

Don't miss the next thrilling installment
of the Faces of Evil series!

# HEINOUS
is coming!

Printed by Amazon Italia Logistica S.r.l.
Torrazza Piemonte (TO), Italy

10363121R00150